SUCH DARLING DODOS

SUCH
DARLING DODOS

and other stories

ANGUS WILSON

SECKER & WARBURG · LONDON

First published in England 1950 by
MARTIN SECKER & WARBURG LIMITED
14 Carlisle Street London W1

© 1950 by Angus Wilson

SBN 436 57509 4

Reprinted 1950, 1954, 1959, 1970

Printed Offset Litho and bound in Great Britain
by Cox & Wyman Ltd,
London, Fakenham and Reading

To

MR. & MRS. PICKERING WALKER

"Rex Imperator" was first published in *Arena*; "Toten-tanz" in *Horizon*, and "What do Hippo's Eat?" in *The Listener*.

CONTENTS

Rex Imperator

THE winter sun poured in through the long french windows of the dining-room. Flames shot up from the burning logs in the hall. In the morning room the coals glowed brightly. But neither sun nor burning wood nor glowing coals could make the house less desolate. Sometimes it seemed that there were too many windows, too much bleak light; at others the house seemed perpetually sombre and dark. But always it was desolate and, above all, expectant. For years now there had been this sense of impending tragedy; the occupants were like passengers in a Railway Waiting Room, idly chattering and frittering away the time. How could they do or say anything positive, for though the crash might be delayed, it would inevitably arrive. To Rex Palmer and his wife, the house was their beloved home and what they feared was disaster, bankruptcy, ruin; but to the family dependants it was a prison against which they chafed, and to which they yet clung for fear of being turned adrift, of having to fend for themselves. They were like parasites washed up by the tide, hanging like limpets to the rock, hating and loathing it, yet waxing fat upon it, devitalizing the air they breathed.

It should have been a prosperous household, for Rex was partner in a well-established firm. To his wife Brenda it was still a source of pride and happiness; though of late even she had begun to feel a strange hopelessness, a fear that Rex could not contrive to pay out for ever to

people who would not help themselves. On a morning
like this when the boys had only just returned to school,
she had to double the energy she put into her housework
in order to avoid depression. To their family dependants
the situation was becoming hateful; they had all three
been there some months now—a longer period than they
had ever known without Rex fulfilling their demands for
money—money which they had almost persuaded themselves was their rightful due, money which would allow
them to return for a space to London and reign supreme
in their own small worlds. They had eaten away at the
foundations until the crumbling edifice shook so that
even *they* were afraid—supposing Rex were to get into
Queer Street, what would become of them? Yet they
were all agreed that it was only his absurd obstinacy that
was at fault—this refusal to sell land because of some
promise to his sons—things were far too immediate for
that sort of sentimental consideration. They had begun
to hate the hand that fed them, the more so that they
could not afford to bite it too hard. Rex they could despise; after all he chose to run the family finances, it was
his fault if there were deficits, besides his temper and
domineering ways cancelled all need for gratitude. But
for Brenda there was nothing left but hatred, she ignored
them so completely, made it so clear that they were there
by Rex's grace not hers. Her courtesy was impassive,
withdrawn, it was quite intolerable, it almost made them
feel guilty.

In so uncongenial an atmosphere it was not surprising
that they clung tenaciously to the outside world, awaited
the morning postal delivery with such eagerness, though

letters came less frequently as the months passed by. But this morning each of them expected not just "letters," but a letter. Brenda's father, Mr. Nicholson, like the brave old sportsman he was, had risked on a horse what little cash he still had from Rex's last loan and had won. It looked as though his luck had changed at last, and he thought lovingly of the thirty quid that was coming, to have a few crisp fivers in his pocket would make him feel a man again. Gwen Rutherford, Rex's sister, was awaiting her alimony. But it was not only the money she expected; after seven years' separation she still believed in that letter from Hugh, that humble, apologetic letter asking her to return; and, now that rumour declared him to have left that common little woman she felt sure that it would come. Rex's brother Basil could hardly expect any actual cash by post, he had long since dried up all sources of financial aid. His sharp eyes however had seen that Rex was wavering over the land sale, soon he would get his money and be free to leave. He had written to a girl in town to put him up—no use in wasting good money on rooms; besides he was sick and tired of the local women, it would be nice to have someone a bit more sophisticated. And now the post was late. They all felt it was really trying them a little *too* high.

If I have to stay in this blasted country,many days more I shall scream, thought Gwen, as the cawing of the rooks circling over the nearby copse reminded her of her remoteness from town. She found Brenda's busy attention to housework more than usually irritating this morning. Not that she was troubled by any con-

scientious feeling that she should lend assistance; but
years of hotel life had allowed her to regard her futile
inactivity as a normal pattern of behaviour, and she had
a vague resentment against her sister-in-law for under-
lining her superfluous position in the household. "I
have never known any house" she used to say "and I've
lived in a good many"—it was true that there were few
boarding houses or private hotels that had not at one
time received her—"where there's so much fuss as this
one. Of course, the trouble is Brenda has no *method*."
She was about to make some criticism of this kind as
she passed through the hall where Brenda was busily
buffeting cushions into shape, but she contented herself
with a snort. "The postal delivery is late again" she
barked. "Yes it is, isn't it?" replied Brenda vaguely,
and as Gwen's broad behind in its tight black cloth
skirt disappeared upstairs, she called "You'll find a
fire in the morning room, dear."

Upstairs in the drawing room rebellion was in full
swing. Old Mr. Nicholson moved aside the screen
with its lotus flowers of beaten copper and put a match
to the fire. "All the damned fires in this house smoke"
he said "I told old Rex at the time that the architect
didn't know his business." Gwen Rutherford did not
reply, she was too busy settling herself on the sofa.
It was a process acquired through years of competition
for the best chairs in private hotel lounges and it took
time. First a place had to be found for Boy, her white
West Highland terrier, then there was her own ample
body to be spread, next she had to put out on the seat
beside her a jade cigarette holder, a shagreen cigarette

case, her knitting and her Boot's library book; she would also have liked the newspaper, but Mr. Nicholson had taken that. She sat bolt upright with her large bust and her short thick arms held defiantly forward. Her fat face with its bulging eyes was blotched from an over-hasty make-up, the lines of her plump cheeks ran in a deep sulk at each side of her small pouting mouth. She looked like the British Bulldog at bay rather than a once beautiful woman soured by seven years of legal separation. Long after most women had grown their hair again, Gwen had retained her peroxide shingle and the rolls of blue stubbled fat at the back of her neck added to the bulldog illusion.

"I know Brenda won't like us using the drawing room in the morning, but I really cannot sit in that depressing morning room," said Gwen. She enumerated each syllable very distinctly in a hard clear voice as though she was being put through a vowel test, though her sentences ended in a whine of self-pity, "Why Rex should have chosen the only room that gets no sun for the morning room I do *not* understand."

"The room would be all right if it had anything like a comfortable seat in it," said Mr. Nicholson as he sank into a deep armchair, dropping cigar ash on one side of him, allowing the newspaper to disintegrate on the other, "Poor old Rex, he's got no sense of comfort, and Brenda's the same, she gets it from her mother, certainly not from me" he chuckled and his small black eyes twinkled with the schoolboy dishonesty that at seventy still disarmed so many hearts and secured so many loans.

Gwen only made a grimacing smile. She disliked and distrusted Mr. Nicholson, and though immediate interests placed them in alliance, she was not prepared to commit herself too far.

Her younger brother Basil stretched out his legs and rested his muddy shoes on the mauve shot-silk cover of another chair. It gave him great pleasure to violate Brenda's beloved drawing room, it was, he felt, almost an aesthetic duty. The winter sun showed up its faded, pastel shabbiness, but its pristine glory must have been almost worse. As a man with an alpha brain and a hard head into the bargain he was able to savour to the full its third-rate pretension. His blood shot blue eyes and his india-rubber features were blurred with amused contempt—the Medici prints, the little silver bowls, the mauve net curtains, the shot-silk covers, the beaten copperware, the chinese lanterns and honesty in pewter mugs—it was all so pathetically genteel and arty. He did not stare long at the room, the light hurt his eyes. He always had a hangover in the mornings now, was always a bit beer-sozzled. He would not have got up so early if he hadn't expected that bloody letter, and now the ruddy post was late. Shutting his eyes, he said "Up the rebels. Workers arise. We *are* in revolution this morning aren't we?" Gwen did not reply. She was always at sea with her brother's open cynicism, though she still believed, or liked to believe, that at thirty-three he would yet startle the world with his brilliance.

Mr. Nicholson did not favour cynicism, indeed sentimental worldliness was his strong suit, but he staked his all on possessing a sense of humour and if an honest Dick Turpin line was called for, he would not refuse it.

"The trouble with us dishonest people, Palmer" he said, "is that we don't know how to be close. Now old Rex is successful because, breathe it not in Gath, he's mean with the shekels. Brenda's the same. That's why they've got money, of course. It always amuses me when old Rex complains of being hard up. Why! they must have a mint of money saved the way they live." It was an unwritten law of the vultures that none of them should ever openly admit to knowing where their victims' money went. "It's beyond me, of course," he went on, "why the hell people should want to save their money up for other people to spend when they're growing daisies. Solomon was a very wise old bird when he said 'A short life and a merry one' or words to that effect. With all my vices I can safely say I've never been mean. My trouble was to stop myself giving it away when I had it. Funny thing I was only thinking this morning of a little Scots girl I lived with—oh way back before you were thought of, in the 'nineties," he bowed old world apology to Gwen for his reference to his mistress, and she smiled back her broadminded permission, "pretty little kid she was, but tough like all Glaswegians. 'Put your money away, Jim,' she said, 'and don't go giving it to Tom, Dick and Harry. They'll no thank ye for it, when ye ha'e none' and she was perfectly right. The only chap who helped me when I was down was poor little Billie Dean, the best lightweight England ever had, and he didn't owe me a sausage. 'Here's a fiver for you, Jimmie, don't say no,' he said,

'You were the only gent of them all who was willing
to know me after I got too old for the ring.' Poor little
blighter, I was always glad I took it, he died a week
later with cancer of the throat." Mr. Nicholson's voice
boomed on in sentimental reminiscence. Mrs. Rutherford
talked in an undertone to Boy, "He likes to sit on the sofa
doesn't he?" she said, "even if his Auntie Brenda is
nasty and fussy about it." Basil dozed off in a half sleep,
his mouth slightly open, he finished an obscene limerick
in Ausonian Latin and thought should he make the
dancing instructress at the Tivoli before he borrowed a
fiver from her or should he borrow the fiver first and
then take her out with it and make her afterwards.

When Mr. Nicholson came to a long pause in his
reminiscence, Gwen seized her opportunity to talk.
The last six or seven years of her life had been so completely blank that she had nothing really to say, so she
always talked of her own immediate movements, making
up by clarity of diction for the lack of content.

"At a quarter past eleven" she said, "I shall go
down to the town for coffee. If you want to come with
me, Basil, I shall be ready at a quarter past eleven. I
shall have to change my library book, this last novel
they gave me is really very dull, so that I shall want to
look in at Boots'. If Brenda wants me to do any shopping
I think I shall do it after coffee, because the Jonquil gets
so crowded. In any case, I shall look in at the Post Office
to complain about the lateness of the post. If Brenda
and Rex won't say anything, I shall have to. But I shall
use their name. 'If it goes on,' I shall say, 'Mr. and Mrs.
Palmer will take it up with the Post Office Headquarters.'

It's only really a question of frightening them. . . ."
While his sister was talking, Basil went to sleep, and
before she had finished, Mr. Nicholson was openly
reading the newspaper. "I hope we shan't sit up late,
because I expect I shall be very tired to-night, I did *not*
sleep well last night." Gwen's mouth snapped tight
as she came to the end of her prospectus of the day, then
she threw away her cigarette, gathered up her belongings,
and followed by Boy she left the room.

Brenda was bending over the sofa in the hall straight-
ening the cushions, so that she almost fell over Gwen's
little dog when it ran straight between her feet. Recover-
ing her balance, she trod on its tail. It let out a yell of
pain and began to emit high, staccato barks.

"Poor Boy" said Gwen, "your Auntie Brenda's so
busy she never saw a poor little dog," and she kissed its
black nose, but Boy refused to be soothed. "I'm so
sorry," mumbled Brenda, but she looked at the trail
of paw marks on the carefully polished parquet floor.
Gwen followed her gaze, "You really ought not to use
such slippery floor polish, Brenda," she remarked,
"someone will break their neck one of these days."
Brenda thought of so much she would like to say, but
she only replied, "I don't think you'd like to see the
floor if it wasn't polished, Gwen." "Of course not,"
said Gwen, speaking even more loudly and distinctly,
as though addressing a child, "It's just a question of
the polish you use, dear. It's worth taking trouble to
get the right kind. It really *is* annoying about the post."
"Perhaps there isn't any post for us to-day," suggested
Brenda. Gwen's mouth went down in an injured pout.

"Of course there is," she snapped, "it's the tenth of the month." Brenda blushed scarlet, she always forgot that wretched alimony. She wished the whole subject didn't embarrass her so, but Gwen seemed to be so proud of being a separated woman, any nice person would have wished to hide it. "I'm so sorry, I quite forgot," but the big orange-flecked face of her sister-in-law seemed to be swelling. Oh dear! thought Brenda, she's going to cry. She tried hard to imagine how awful it must be to have married Hugh Rutherford so that she could sympathize, but she knew very well she would never have married such a man, and if she had, she felt sure she would have held him. She could never get used to tears from so big a woman and in the morning too, when there was so much to do. But Gwen's tears were deflected by a sudden, trickling noise. The sisters-in-law looked down to see Boy's leg lifted high against the sofa. "Oh, you wretched dog," Brenda was really dismayed. Gwen picked up the little white-haired squirming animal, "Naughty boy" she said, "where are your manners?" and she tapped him on the nose. "I didn't mean to do it, Auntie Brenda," she added in a baby lisp and then in her own clear enunciation. "Anyhow there's nothing that can't be cleared up in a minute. Come along, Boy we're in disgrace, we'll go and powder our noses."

Brenda tried to dissipate her anger by dusting Rex's cups that he had won at school. He had been such a wonderful athlete, it had always made her proud to touch them, they looked so fine shining against the mahogany sideboard.

"Careful with the Lares, Brenda dear," said Basil, as he made his way upstairs. That damned bitch hadn't written and the pubs weren't open until twelve. He would go to his room and get on with that translation of "The Frogs." Bloody hell! he was a first-rate scholar *and* he'd knocked about a bit, just the man for Aristophanes. He'd astonish them with the finished article. "Mr. Palmer has given us a translation as accurate as any University don can demand and as witty as a West End revue." But Basil knew that the tooth glass would be there and the remains of a bottle of whisky, the morning was a bloody awful time to be up, best to lie down and then if he could get that girl at the dance hall a bit canned, well he might . . . yes, there was always something to think about.

"I don't think Elsie's done your room yet, Basil!" Brenda called after him, but he affected not to hear. He'd lie in his shoes on the unmade bed, it was almost more than she could bear. She had tried so hard to share Rex's admiration for his brother, but if he was so clever why didn't he do something instead of sponging on Rex and being beastly and sarcastic all the time. Rex said Basil had been embittered by the way the college had treated him in taking away that lectureship, but people had no right to go on sulking like that. It had been so lovely going up to Cambridge with Rex to his old college, he had seemed so popular with the dons— the best athlete the college had known, the master had said. She felt again the shape of that long muslin dress she had worn, shell pink it had been with a white satin princess petticoat. Rex had looked so handsome in his morning coat. He had shown her the Judas Tree in King's College garden, and she had won his praise when she had pointed out the thick cream colour of the magnolia flowers. "I never knew how beautiful Cambridge was until I saw it through my wife's eyes," he had said to his tutor. Now they could go there no more, because Rex had written so sharply after Basil's dismissal.

Dog hair on the sofa, bootmarks on the chair covers, cigar smoke pervading the air, ash and newspapers all over the floor. This is my drawing room, thought Brenda, as she came in from the hall, and she straightened her back to control her rising hysteria. Suddenly she detected a smell of burning. Her father had gone to sleep and his cigar stump had set light to the little marqueterie table. "Oh father really," was all she said, as she put out the smouldering wood. Mr. Nicholson awoke with a start, "Sorry, girlie," he said, "I must have dropped off. Has the post come yet?" he asked, and a wave of self-pity came over him as he thought of himself, a lonely old man who'd lived like a prince, reduced to worrying whether some twopenny-half-penny bookie had sent a paltry tenner. "There doesn't seem to be any post," said Brenda in a flat voice. Mr. Nicholson looked up. "You sound tired, girlie. I don't know what old Rex is about letting you do all this housework." Brenda never attended to what her father said; after so many years of trying not to dislike and despise, she found it easier to forget him. "I'm all right, thank you," she replied. "If it's cash young master Rex is keeping you short of, I hope I'll be able to help you in a few days. I'm expecting a fairly large cheque, but at the moment I'm stony broke." Brenda never bothered to consider her father's words in relation to their truth, but she knew very well the pattern of his mind. "I think I can spare you some money, only you are not to worry Rex." "That's very good of you, girlie, I don't like to take it." "It's quite all right. I'd rather do anything than have you worry Rex." Brenda's honesty did not allow her to be gracious in making loans, her father knew why she was giving him the money, so that she saw no sense in pretending to motives of filial affection. "Will ten pounds be enough?" she asked. Cheated of his sentimental scene, Mr. Nicholson was not prepared to be accommodating. "Better make it twenty," he said. "Very well," said Brenda, "I'll give you a cheque."

Neither porridge nor tea seemed to take the bitterness from Rex's mouth, and his head ached more painfully than it had before he got up. He swallowed two aspirins and decided to go out into the grounds. He walked down the side of the house past the rock garden. It looked so bare and pathetic in winter, but he anticipated with pleasure the masses of aubrietia, crimson, lavender, blue that would blaze there in May. The lily pond, too, looked dismal with the pale reflection of the winter sun, only three goldfish had survived last month's ice. He felt happy, however, just to be alive here in the garden that was his own and then—suddenly he stepped out through the path in the wood on to the paddock and he felt quite sick. This was the beginning of the land he had bought for his sons, and there, at the far end, tossing their manes, as they ambled after one another, were

Polly and Ginger. There would be no riding next holidays, he did not know how he would be able to tell the boys. In the foreground the cumbrous, grey sheep moved slowly, cropping the grass. He had been so pleased to allow Duckett the use of the pasture— "doing the squire" Basil would have called it—and now he must tell him to find some other field. "To-morrow to fresh woods and pastures new." "The swollen sheep look up and are not fed." Well his family could never say that; if *they* were swollen, he thought savagely, it was because they fed so well at his expense. He definitely would not sell, he would tell them so to-day. "They must look after themselves," he said aloud, but as he spoke the words he knew that the fate of his sons' land was sealed.

Gwen and Mr. Nicholson were regretting the passing of the old West End when Rex came into the room. He had never cared for London, and since his family had wasted their money there, his hostility to the metropolis was almost pathological. He knew the pattern of this conversation so well, Gwen describing the gaiety of the "'twenties," Mr. Nicholson countering with the stories of "'nineties" night life, each outboasting the other, each hoping that he would be duly abashed at being so provincial. In his present frame of mind it made him feel almost murderous.

"My dear young woman," Mr. Nicholson was saying, "There *were* no music hall artists after Marie Lloyd. I'll never forget going with her to see one of these damned revues just before she died. 'Take me out, Jimmie,' she said, 'This is way above my station.' Poor old

Marie, she never pretended to be anything but what she was, but I don't suppose there was a bigger-hearted woman living. . . ." But here Gwen saw her chance. "Well, of course," she said, "I'm not old enough to remember much about Marie Lloyd, but I'm sure no actress can have been more generous than Florence Mills. What a wonderful show that was! Of course, there's no doubt that the coloured people have us completely beaten where dancing is in question. *You* remember Blackbirds, Rex," she said, turning to her brother "or you ought to, we all went together that evening Hugh was so squiffy."

"There were so many evenings when Hugh was squiffy," said Rex savagely. "At the moment, Gwen, I'm not very good at remembering." He squared his shoulders and with a certain air of drama, "I imagine you'll be interested to hear I've decided to sell the land" he announced.

Mr. Nicholson was not apparently very interested, as soon as he felt sure that he would get the money, he preferred to regard the whole transaction as not affecting him. "You've done quite right, Rex, old boy, I'm sure," he said in an offhand manner, and was about to resume his discussion, but Gwen was less subtle. "Thank goodness you've thought of your family at last," she said firmly, and she was about to release her feelings of the last few weeks when a certain flush in her brother's features made her pause. There were very few things that made Gwen Rutherford think twice, indeed thinking at all was by now an artificial process to her, and in general she believed in treating her brother's bad temper with sledgehammer firmness. Suddenly, however, as she looked now, she saw a little boy in Etons, his face flushed purple, driving the point of a pair of scissors into his nurse's hand, and again she remembered an older boy, almost sixteen, pounding and hitting at Basil's face on the green turf of the Downs, by the cliff edge where, far below, the Channel tossed grey and green. Such visual memories were so rare to Gwen that she stifled her words and sat back, her fat face puffed and trembling with the pent-up indignation she had so nearly released.

When Basil came into the room they were all silent, almost brooding, "Good God!" he said, "the last day in the old home, eh?" "You're nearer than you think," replied Rex, "I've decided to sell the land." Basil's heart pounded with pleasure at his brother's humiliation, but now was not the moment to rub salt into the wound, so he changed the subject. "Seen anything of the post, Rex?" he said. "Yes." Gwen took up the tale. "I've been asking Brenda all the morning. It's most inconvenient." "I suppose it's never occurred to you that Brenda might find your continuous grumbling inconvenient," said Rex, his neck swelling over his collar. "No," said Gwen, her mouth snapping in fury, "it hasn't." "Well, it's time it did," said Rex, his voice high with hysteria. Basil cupped his hands behind his head and leant back in the armchair, He gazed at his brother fixedly, "Poor old Rex, you don't like not being lord of the manor any more one bit, do you?" Rex strode across and stood over Basil, "You'll bloody well leave first thing to-morrow," he said. "You produce the money," laughed Basil, "and you won't see me for dust." Rex's clenched hands came up above his brother's face, Gwen gave a little scream. But any violence was avoided by Brenda's entrance. "Here's the post at last," she said, and, going up to her husband, she handed him a packet of letters. Rex's quick gaze caught sight of envelopes addressed to Basil, Gwen, Mr. Nicholson —and for himself, bills, bills. "Can you see my letter from the solicitors?" said Gwen quickly. "I think there ought to be one for me, Rex old boy," said Mr. Nicholson. They both spoke at once. "Yes," replied Rex in scarcely audible tones, "your letters are here," then suddenly his voice rose as it trembled with rage, "Whether you'll get them is another question. I decide what happens to letters that come into this house." "My God, you bloody, spoilt, little fool," shouted Basil, but he had allowed his genuine contempt to show at an unfortunate moment. Rex's colour flushed to scarlet, and his face fell on one side as though with a paralytic stroke, a fallen lump of twitching, scarlet flesh from which a dark eye stared wildly like a runaway horse's. He began to tear the letters into small pieces. Brenda's face was sorrowful, yet triumphant for her poor, unhappy, violent boy who was master of them all. Mr. Nicholson found no means to move, his age told against him when force was needed, and he fell back on internal self-pity. Gwen's heavy mass melted into tears. Basil alone, his jealousy and hatred of his brother bursting through his decayed faculties, took action. He seized Rex's hands, trying to prise the fragments of paper from the hysterically clenched fingers, but Rex's

superior strength soon told, and pushing Basil to one
side he sent him sprawling across the floor, scattering
and breaking Brenda's little black china bowl of roses,
with its kingfisher centre-piece. Turning sharply round,
Rex flung the pieces of the letters into the fire. "That's
where you can get your letters from, if you've got the
nerve," he screamed, "I'll teach you to write whining
to people outside. *I* provide for the family and in
future you'll please remember that." Burying his head
in his arms, he leant on the mantelpiece and began to
sob.

The noise of her beloved objects breaking and the
realization that Rex's triumph had turned to tears roused
Brenda into action. "You'll be late for coffee, if you
don't go soon," she said, in her flat voice, "would you
remember to get some cakes in the town, Gwen, please.
You'd better go too, father, you know you don't like
to trust anyone else to change your library book." She
ignored Basil as he rose from the floor, but she put her
arm round her husband's waist. "Can you spare a minute,
Rex darling," she said, "to look at the cistern. Cook
and I have been doing our best with it, but it needs a
man's hand."

A Little Companion

THEY say in the village that Miss Arkwright has never been the same since the war broke out, but she knows that it all began a long time before that—on 24th July, 1936, to be exact, the day of her forty-seventh birthday.

She was in no way a remarkable person. Her appearance was not particularly distinguished and yet she was without any feature that could actively displease. She had enough personal eccentricities to fit into the pattern of English village life, but none so absurd or anti-social that they could embarrass or even arouse gossip beyond what was pleasant to her neighbours. She accepted her position as an old maid with that cheerful good humour and occasional irony which are essential to English spinsters since the deification of Jane Austen, or more sacredly Miss Austen, by the upper middle classes, and she attempted to counteract the inadequacy of the unmarried state by quiet, sensible and tolerant social work in the local community. She was liked by nearly everyone, though she was not afraid of making enemies where she knew that her broad but deeply felt religious principles were being opposed. Any socially pretentious or undesirably extravagant conduct, too, was liable to call forth from her an unexpectedly caustic and well-aimed snub. She was invited everywhere and always accepted the invitations. You could see her at every tea or cocktail party, occasionally drinking a third gin,

but never more. Quietly but well dressed, with one or
two very fine old pieces of jewellery that had come
down to her from her grandmother, she would pass
from one group to another, laughing or serious as the
occasion demanded. She smoked continuously her own,
rather expensive, brand of cigarettes—"My one vice"
she used to say "the only thing that stands between me
and secret drinking." She listened with patience, but
with a slight twinkle in the eye, to Mr. Hodgson's endless
stories of life in Dar-Es-Salaam or Myra Hope's breathless
accounts of her latest system of diet. John Hobday in
his somewhat ostentatiously gentleman-farmer attire
would describe his next novel about East Anglian life
to her before even his beloved daughter had heard of it.
Richard Trelawney, just down from Oxford, found
that she had read and really knew Donne's sermons,
yet she could swop detective stories with Colonel
Wright by the hour, and was his main source for quotations when *The Times* crossword was in question. She
it was who incorporated little Mrs. Grantham into
village life, when that rather underbred, suburban
woman came there as Colonel Grantham's second wife,
checking her vulgar remarks about "the lower classes"
with kindly humour, but defending her against the
formidable battery of Lady Vernon's antagonism. Yet
she it was also who was first at Lady Vernon's when
Sir Robert had his stroke and her unobtrusive kindliness
and real services gained her a singular position behind
the grim reserve of the Vernon family. She could always
banter the vicar away from his hobby horse of the
Greek rite when at parish meetings the agenda seemed

to have been buried for ever beneath a welter of Eucho-
logia and Menaia. She checked Sir Robert's anti-
bolshevik phobia from victimizing the County Librarian
for her Fabianism, but was fierce in her attack on the
local council when she thought that class prejudice had
prevented Commander Osborne's widow from getting
a council house. She led in fact an active and useful
existence, yet when anyone praised her she would only
laugh—"My dear," she would say "hard work's the
only excuse old maids like me have got for existing at
all, and even then I don't know that they oughtn't to
lethalize the lot of us." As the danger of war grew
nearer in the 'thirties her favourite remark was "Well,
if they've got any sense this time they'll keep the young
fellows at home and put us useless old maids in the
trenches," and she said it with real conviction.

With her good carriage, ample figure and large, deep
blue eyes, she even began to acquire a certain beauty
as middle age approached. People speculated as to why
she had never married. She had in fact refused a number
of quite personable suitors. The truth was that from
girlhood she had always felt a certain repulsion from
physical contact. Not that she was in any way prudish,
she was remarkable for a rather eighteenth-century turn
of coarse phrase, indeed verbal freedom was the easier
for her in that sexual activity was the more remote. Nor
would psychoanalysts have found anything of particular
interest in her; she had no abnormal desires, as a child
she had never felt any wish to change her sex or observed
any peculiarly violent or crude incident that could have
resulted in what is called a psychic trauma. She just

wasn't interested, and was perhaps as a result a little
over-given to talking of "all this fuss and nonsense
that's made over sex." She would however have liked
to have had a child. She recognized this as a common
phenomenon among childless women and accepted it,
though she could never bring herself to admit it openly
or laugh about it in the commonsensical way in which
she treated her position as an old maid. As the middle
years approached she found a sudden interest and even
sometimes a sudden jealousy over other people's babies
and children growing upon her, attacking her unexpectedly and with apparent irrelevancy to time or place.
She was equally wide-awake to the dangers of the late
forties and resolutely resisted such foolish fancies, though
she became as a result a little snappish and over-gruff
with the very young. "Now, my dear," she told herself
"you *must* deal with this nonsense or you'll start getting
odd." How very odd she could not guess.

The Granthams always gave a little party for her on
her birthdays. "Awful nonsense at my age" she had
been saying now for many years "but I never say no to
a drink." Her forty-seventh birthday party was a particular success; Mary Hatton was staying with the Granthams
and like Miss Arkwright she was an ardent Janeite so
they'd been able to talk Mr. Collins and Mrs. Elton and
the Elliots to their hearts' content, then Colonel Grantham had given her some tips about growing meconopsis
and finally Mrs. Osborne had been over to see the new
rector at Longhurst, so they had a good-natured but
thoroughly enjoyable "cat" about the state of the
rectory there. She was just paying dutiful attention to

her hostess' long complaint about the grocery deliveries, preparatory to saying good-bye, when suddenly a thin, whining, but remarkably clear, child's voice said loudly in her ear "Race you home, Mummy." She looked around her in surprise, then decided that her mind must have wandered from the boring details of Mrs. Grantham's saga, but almost immediately the voice sounded again "Come on, Mummy, you are a slowcoach, I said 'race you home'." This time Miss Arkwright was seriously disturbed, she wondered if Colonel Grantham's famous high spirits had got the better of him, but it could hardly have been so, she thought as she saw his face earnest in conversation—"The point is, Vicar, not so much whether we want to intervene as whether we've got to." She began to feel most uncomfortable and as soon as politeness allowed she made her way home.

The village street seemed particularly hot and dusty, the sunlight on the whitewashed cottages peculiarly glaring as she walked along. "One too many on a hot day that's your trouble, my dear" she said to herself and felt comforted by so material an explanation. The familiar trimness of her own little house and the cool shade of the walnut tree on the front lawn further calmed her nerves. She stopped for a moment to pick up a basket of lettuce that old Pyecroft had left at the door and then walked in. After the sunlight outside, the hall seemed so dark that she could hardly discern even the shape of the grandfather clock. Out of this shadowy blackness came the child's voice loudly and clearly but if anything more nasal than before. "Beat you to it this time" it said. Miss Arkwright's heart stopped for a moment and her lungs seemed to contract and then almost instantaneously she had seen it—a little white-faced boy, thin, with matchstick arms and legs growing out of shrunken clothes, with red-rimmed eyes and an adenoidal open-mouthed expression. Instantaneously, because the next moment he was not there, almost like a flickering image against the eye's retina. Miss Arkwright straightened her back, took a deep breath, then she went upstairs, took off her shoes and lay down on her bed.

It was many weeks before anything fresh occurred and she felt happily able to put the whole incident down to cocktails and the heat, indeed she began to remember that she had woken next morning with a severe headache —"You're much too old to start suffering from hang-overs" she told herself. But the next experience was really more alarming. She had been up to London to buy a wedding present at Harrods and, arriving some-what late for the returning train, found herself sitting in a stuffy and overpacked carriage. She felt therefore particularly pleased to see the familiar slate quarries that heralded the approach of Brankston Station, when suddenly a sharp dig drove the bones of her stays into her ribs. She looked with annoyance at the woman next to her—a blowsy creature with feathers in her hat —when she saw to her surprise that the woman was quietly asleep, her arms folded in front of her. Then in her ears there sounded "Chuff, Chuff, Chuff, Chuff," followed by a little snort and a giggle, and then quite unmistakably the whining voice saying "Rotten old

train." After that it seemed to her as though for a few
moments pandemonium had broken loose in the carriage
—shouts and cries and a monotonous thumping against
the woodwork as though someone were beating an
impatient rhythm with their foot—yet no other occupant
seemed in the slightest degree disturbed. They were
for Miss Arkwright moments of choking and agonizing
fear. She dreaded that at any minute the noise would
grow so loud that the others would notice, for she felt
an inescapable responsibility for the incident; yet had
the whole carriage risen and flung her from the window
as a witch it would in some degree have been a release
from the terrible sense of personal obsession, it would
have given objective reality to what now seemed an
uncontrollable expansion of her own consciousness
into space, it would at the least have shown that others
were mad beside herself. But no slightest ripple broke
the drowsy torpor of the hot carriage in the August sun.
She was deeply relieved when the train at last drew into
Brankston and the impatience of her invisible attendant
was assuaged, but no sooner had she set foot on the
platform than she heard once more the almost puling
whine, the too familiar "Race you home, Mummie."
She knew then that whatever it was, it had come to stay,
that her homecomings would no longer be to the
familiar comfort of her house and servants, but that there
would always be a childish voice, a childish face to greet
her for one moment as she crossed the threshold.

And so it proved. Gradually at first, at more than
weekly intervals, and then increasingly, so that even a
short spell in the vegetable garden or with the rock

plants would mean impatient whining, wanton scattering of precious flowers, overturning of baskets—and then that momentary vision, lengthened now sometimes to five minutes' duration, that sickly, cretinous face. The very squalor of the child's appearance was revolting to Miss Arkwright, for whom cheerful, good health was the first of human qualities. Sometimes the sickliness of the features would be of the thick, flaccid, pasty appearance that suggested rich feeding and late hours, and then the creature would be dressed in a velvet suit and fauntleroy collar that might have clothed an over-indulged French *bourgeois* child; at other times the appearance was more cretinous, adenoidal and emaciated, and then it would wear the shrunken uniform and thick black boots of an institution idiot. In either case it was a child quite out of keeping with the ·home it sought to possess—a home of quiet beauty, unostentatious comfort and restrained good taste. Of course, Miss Arkwright argued, it was an emanation from the sick side of herself so that it was bound to be diseased, but this realization did not compensate for dribble marks on her best dresses or for sticky finger marks on her tweed skirts.

At first she tried to ignore the obsession with her deep reserve of stoic patience, but as it continued, she felt the need of the Church. She became a daily communicant and delighted the more "spikey" of her neighbours. She prayed ceaselessly for release or resignation. A lurking sense of sin was roused in her and she wondered if small frivolities and pleasures were the cause of her visitation; she remembered that after all it had

first begun when she was drinking gin. Her religion
had always been of the "brisk" and "sensible" variety,
but now she began to fear that she had been over-
suspicious of "enthusiasm" or "pietism." She gave up
all but the most frugal meals, distributed a lot of her
clothes to the poor, slept on a board and rose at one
in the morning to say a special Anglican office from a
little book she had once been given by a rather despised
High Church cousin. The only result seemed to be to
cause scandal to her comfortable, old-fashioned parlour-
maid and cook. She mentioned her state of sin in general
terms to the vicar and he lent her Neale's translations
of the Coptic and Nestorian rites, but they proved of
little comfort. At Christmas she rather shamefacedly
and secretively placed a little bed with a richly filled
stocking in the corner of her bedroom, but the child
was not to be blackmailed. Throughout the day she
could hear faint but unsavoury sounds of uncontrolled
and slovenly guzzling, like the distant sound, of pigs
feeding, and when evening came she was pursued by ever
louder retching and the disturbing smell of vomit.

On Boxing Day she visited her old and sensible friend
the bishop and told him the whole story. He looked at
her very steadily with the large, dramatic brown eyes that
were so telling in the pulpit, and for a long time he remained silent. Miss Arkwright hoped that he would
advise her quickly, for she could feel a growing tugging
at her skirt. It was obvious that this quiet, spacious
library was no place for a child, and she could not have
borne to see these wonderful, old books disturbed even
if she was the sole observer of the sacrilege. At last the

bishop spoke. "You say that the child appears ill and depraved, has this evil appearance been more marked in the last weeks?" Miss Arkwright was forced to admit that it had. "My dear old friend" said the bishop and he put his hand on hers. "It is your sick self that you are seeing, and all this foolish abstinence, this extravagant martyrdom are making you more sick." The bishop was a great Broad Churchman of the old school. "Go out into the world and take in its beauty and its colour. Enjoy what is yours and thank God for it." And without more ado, he persuaded Miss Arkwright to go to London for a few weeks.

Established at Berners', she set out to have a good time. She was always fond of expensive meals, but her first attempt to indulge at Claridge's proved an appalling failure, for with every course the voice grew louder and louder in her ears, "Coo! what rotten stuff," it kept on repeating, "I want an ice." Henceforth her meals were taken almost exclusively on Selfridge's roof or in ice-cream parlours, an unsatisfying and indigestible diet. Visits to the theatre were at first a greater success, she saw the new adaptation of "The Mill on the Floss," and a version of "Lear" modelled on the original Kean production. The child had clearly never seen a play before and was held entranced by the mere spectacle. But soon it began to grow restless, a performance of "Hedda Gabbler" was entirely ruined by rustlings, kicks, whispers, giggles and a severe bout of hiccoughs. For a time it was kept quiet by musical comedies and farces, but in the end Miss Arkwright found herself attending only "Where the Rainbow Ends," "Mother Goose" and "Buckie's Bears"

—it was not a sophisticated child. As the run of Christmas plays drew near their end she became desperate, and one afternoon she left a particularly dusty performance at the Circus and visited her old friend Madge Cleaver—once again to tell all. "Poor Bessie" said Madge Cleaver and she smiled so spiritually, "How real Error can seem," for Madge was a Christian Scientist. "But it's so *un*real, dear, if we can only have the courage to see the Truth. Truth denies Animal Magnetism, Spiritualism and all other false manifestations." She lent Miss Arkwright *Science and Health* and promised that she would give her "absent treatment."

At first Miss Arkwright felt most comforted. Mrs. Eddy's denial of the reality of most common phenomena and in particular of those that are evil seemed to offer a way out. Unfortunately, the child seemed quite unconvinced of its own non-existence. One afternoon Miss Arkwright thought with horror that by adopting a theology that denied the existence of Matter and gave reality only to Spirit she might well be gradually removing herself from the scene, whilst leaving the child in possession. After all her own considerable bulk was testimony enough to her material nature, whilst the child might well in some repulsive way be accounted spirit. Terrified by the prospect before her, she speedily renounced Christian Science.

She returned to her home and by reaction decided to treat the whole phenomenon on the most material basis possible. She submitted her body to every old-fashioned purgative, she even indulged in a little amateur bloodletting, for might not the creature be some ill humour or

sickly emanation of the body itself? But this anti-
quarian leechcraft only produced serious physical weak-
ness and collapse. She was forced to call in Dr. Kent who
at once terminated the purgatives and put her on to port
wine and beefsteak.

Failure of material remedies forced Miss Arkwright
at last to a conviction which she had feared from the
start. The thing, she decided, must be a genuine psychic
phenomenon. It cost her much to admit this for she had
always been very contemptuous of spiritualism, and
regarded it as socially undesirable where it was not
consciously fraudulent. But she was by now very desperate and willing to waive the deepest prejudices to free
herself from the vulgar and querulous apparition. For a
month or more she attended seances in London, but
though she received "happy" communications from
enough small Indian or Red Indian children to have
started a nursery school, no medium or clairvoyant
could tell her anything that threw light on her little
companion. At one of the seances, however, she met a
thin, red-haired, pre-Raphaelite sort of lady in a long grey
garment and sandals, who asked her to attend the Circle
of the Seventh Pentacle in the Earllands Road. The
people she found there did not attract Miss Arkwright;
she decided that the servants of the Devil were either
common frauds or of exceedingly doubtful morals, but
the little group was enthusiastic when she told her story—
How could she hope to fight such Black Powers, they
asked, unless she was prepared to invoke the White Art?
Although she resisted their arguments at first, she finally
found herself agreeing to a celebration of the Satanic

Mass in her own home. She sent cook and Annie away for a week and prepared to receive the Circle. Their arrival in the village caused a great stir, partly because of their retinue of goats and rabbits. It had been decided that Miss Arkwright should celebrate the mass herself, an altar had been set up in the drawing room, she had bought an immense white maternity gown from Debenham's and had been busy all the week learning her words, but at the last minute something within her rebelled, she could not bring herself to say the Lord's Prayer backwards and the Mass had to be called off. In the morning the devotees of the Pentacle left with many recriminations. The only result seemed to be that valuable ornaments were missing from the bedrooms occupied by the less reputable, whilst about those rooms in which the Devil's true servants had slept there hung an odour of goat that no fumigation could remove.

Miss Arkwright had long since given up visiting her neighbours, though they had not ceased to speculate about her. A chance remark that she had "two now to provide for," had led them to think that she believed herself pregnant. After this last visitation Lady Vernon decided that the time had come to act. She visited Miss Arkwright early one morning, and seeing the maternity gown which was still lying in the sitting room, she was confirmed in her suspicions. "Bessie dear," she said. "You've got to realize that you're seriously ill, mentally ill," and she packed Miss Arkwright off to a brain specialist in Welbeck Street. This doctor, finding nothing physically wrong, sent her to a psychoanalyst. Poor Miss Arkwright! She was so convinced of her own insanity,

that she could think of no argument if they should wish
to shut her up. But the analyst, a smart, grey-haired Jew,
laughed when she murmured "madness." "We don't
talk in those terms any more, Miss Arkwright. You're a
century out of date. It's true there are certain disturbingly
psychotic features in what you tell me, but nothing, I
think, that won't yield to deep analysis," and deep
analysis she underwent for eight months or more, busily
writing down dreams at night and lying on a couch
"freely associating" by day. At the end of that time the
analyst began to form a few conclusions. "The child
itself," he said, "is unimportant, the fact that you still
see it even less so. What is important is that you now
surround yourself with vulgarity and whining. You
have clearly a need for these things which you have
inhibited too long in an atmosphere of refinement."
It was decided that Miss Arkwright should sublimate
this need by learning thé saxophone. Solemnly each
day the poor lady sat in the drawing room—that room
which had resounded with Bach and Mozart—and
practised the altsax. At last one day when she had got
so far as to be able to play the opening bars of "Alligator
Stomp," her sense of the ridiculous rebelled and she
would play no more, though her little companion showed
great restlessness at the disappearance of noises which
accorded all too closely with its vulgar taste.

I shall treat myself, she decided, and after long
thought she came to the conclusion that the most
salient feature of the business lay in the child's constant
reiteration of the challenge, "Race you home, Mummie";
with this it had started and with this it had continued.

If, thought Miss Arkwright, I were to leave home completely, not only this house, but also England, then perhaps it would withdraw its challenge and depart.

In January, 1938, then, she set out on her travels. All across Europe, in museums and cafés and opera houses, it continued to throw down the gauntlet—"Race you home, Mummie," and there it would be in her hotel bedroom. It seemed, however, anxious to take on local colour and would appear in a diversity of national costumes, often reviving for the purpose peasant dresses seen only at folk-dance festivals or when worn by beggars in order to attract tourists. For Miss Arkwright this rather vulgar and commercial World's Fair aspect of her life was particularly distressing. The child also attempted to alter its own colour, pale brown it achieved in India, in China a faint tinge of lemon, and in America by some misunderstanding of the term Red Indian it emerged bright scarlet. She was especially horrified by the purple swelling with which it attempted to emulate the black of the African natives. But whatever its colour, it was always there.

At last the menace of war in September found Miss Arkwright in Morroco and along with thousands of other British travellers she hurried home, carrying, she felt, her greatest menace with her. It was only really after Munich that she became reconciled to its continued presence, learning gradually to incorporate its noises, its appearance, its whole personality into her daily life. She went out again among her neighbours and soon everyone had forgotten that she had ever been ill. It was true that she was forced to address her companion occasionally with a word of conciliation, or to administer a slap in its direction when it was particularly provoking, but she managed to disguise these peculiarities beneath her normal gestures.

One Saturday evening in September, 1939, she was returning home from the rectory, worried by the threat of approaching war and wondering how she could best use her dual personality to serve her country, when she was suddenly disturbed to hear a clattering of hoofs and a thunderous bellow behind her. She turned to see at some yards distance a furious bull, charging down the village street. She began immediately to run for her home, the little voice whining in her ear "Race you home, Mummie." But the bull seemed to gain upon her, and in her terror she redoubled her speed, running as she had not run since she was a girl. She heard, it is true, a faint sighing in her ears as of dying breath, but she was too frightened to stop until she was safe at her own door. In she walked and, to her amazement, indeed, to her horror, look where she would, the little child was *not* there. She had taken up his challenge to a race and she had won.

She lay in bed that night depressed and lonely. She realized only too clearly that difficult as it was to get rid of him—now that the child was gone she found herself thinking of "him" rather than "it"—it would be well-nigh impossible to get him back. The sirens that declared war next morning seemed only a confirmation of her personal loss. She went into mourning and rarely emerged from the house. For a short while it is true, her spirits were revived when the evacuee children came from the East End, some of the more cretinous and adenoidal seemed curiously like her lost one. But country air and food soon gave them rosy cheeks and sturdy legs and she rapidly lost her interest. Before the year was out she was almost entirely dissociated from the external world, and those few friends, who found time amid the cares of war to visit her in her bedroom, decided that there was little that could be done for one who showed so little response. The vicar, who was busy translating St. Gregory Nazianzen's prayers for victory, spoke what was felt to be the easiest and kindest verdict when he described her as "just another war casualty."

Learning's Little Tribute

AS soon as the clergyman had murmured his last word over the coffin, Miss Wells was scuttling with almost unseemly haste down the yew-lined avenue towards the cemetery gates. It was one of her misfortunes that, though well equipped with the proper rules of conduct in life, she too often spoiled their effect in her anxiety to show her knowledge of them. It was right, of course, to leave the relatives to their private grief, but not perhaps at the double. Her haste was, however, dictated in part by the extreme cold, for though a glorious sunny day for January there was yet a bitter east wind and Miss Wells was above everything delicate. In part also she was genuinely moved to tears; she had not known Hugh Craddock well—just the ordinary requests for her services in typing and proof-reading—but the thought that he had died with his contribution to the great work still unfinished and the sight of the other encyclopaedists gathered round the graveside, so noble, yet themselves no longer young and all too liable to be snatched away, were overmuch for her susceptible emotions. The little bows and ribbons with which she was decorated shook and trembled, the lucky charm bracelets and semi-precious necklaces jangled as she searched among the debris of memo notes, lipstick ends and loose powder for her lace-bordered handkerchief. Who, she wondered, could possibly take over "Art" now that Mr. Craddock was gone?

The same question was disturbing Dr. Earley, the assistant editor, as with solemn but springy steps he walked along the gravel pathway in conversation with the chief, attentive and deferential as befitted a subordinate, yet independent and forceful as was correct for an up and coming figure in the world of popular scholarship.

"It isn't easy, Brunton" he said, and his voice with its over-elocutionized vowels ill-concealing their Cockney origin sounded like some nineteenth-century roadside preacher, "to think of the world without Hugh Craddock. So modest and unobtrusive," even at such a time he found it difficult to use these words without a slight note of contempt "yet so painstaking and devoted a scholar. But however little we may wish to do so" and here he felt himself free to resume a more jolly ringing confident tone, less denominational, more that of the popular lay radio preacher "we have to think of the living— of those who are left behind, of his family, and of what —and perhaps only those of us who are scholars can understand this—was as dear to him as any wife or child, his work upon the Encyclopaedia. Poor Craddock! Thank God that a few of us at least were privileged to know something of what he proposed to do had he been spared."

Mr. Brunton's sharp little eyes glanced cynically for a moment from his heavy blue-jowled face.

"Yes, Earley" he said bitterly "I shall have to think of the living, I have indeed already done so. But for the moment, if you please, I would like to allow my thoughts to remain with the dead."

The bitter east wind seemed to cut through all the warm pullovers with which his valet had provided him, through all the comfortable layers of fat which protected his body. Neither his wealth nor his everyday, jog-along common sense were sufficient guards against fears of mortality in such a setting. Never had he felt so cynical and contemptuous towards his subordinates, never so bitterly aware of the paltry nature of his "scholarly" hobby. He almost regretted that his autocratic character had prevented him from investing in some enterprise of real learning, even though he would have been forced to assume a less dominant role. At such a moment he felt painfully conscious of the truth of that title of the "Maecenas of Hacks" which his enemies had given him. The quick intelligence which had brought him to the front rank of commerce had always prevented him from taking at their own valuation the imitation scholars with whom he had surrounded himself in launching *The People's History of the World*, the *Digest of Great Sayings*, and now *The Universal Encyclopaedia of the Humanities*; but to-day at the grave of the only one of them for whom he had felt any respect and with the clay and worms of his own flesh threatening him so disturbingly, he was ready to bark and bluster at these self-deceiving, ambitious shams as he would at any secretary or clerk in his great City offices. At the sight of Miss Wells' tearful features, however, he softened. Her pathetic, disinterested belief in the great work for which she was proud to act as general dog's-body could only arouse an amused pity.

"Now don't you catch cold, Miss Wells, one corpse

is enough for to-day, you know" he said and moved by the shocked convention, which she tried to conceal out of deference for his greatness, he added "Poor Craddock, I should be content if I thought we could any of us know one-tenth of the happiness that *he* got from his work."

"Ah! yes, indeed. That at least must be a comfort to us."

Dr. Earley's unctuous Cockney whine broke into his chief's words, as the canting tones of some Puritan divine must often have broken into Cromwell's reflections and with much the same effect.

"I was thinking the same thing myself as I stood by the graveside of our dear friend, and listened to those simple old words which were yet so poignant, perhaps *because* of their very simplicity, perhaps *because* we have heard them so often. We have suffered a great loss. But he? I wonder. He lived so much in the world of beauty, among his pictures and his cathedrals. No. I don't think he will suffer much from the loss of mere material things. Except of course" he added hurriedly "the separation from his dear ones. And them" he took Miss Wells' hand and assured any possible doubts that might beset her by the steady gaze of his clear blue eyes, "and them he will see again."

It was typical of Dr. Earley that he should so soon cut across his chief's mood again. The dramatic possibilities of the occasion were more than he could bear to forego. Though he had forsaken the cruder aspects of nonconformity for a wider, more all-embracing transcendentalism—he called it Christian humanism—as his devotion to the great heritage of English letters

had advanced him in the social scale, there were still two
Chadband marks upon him—his morbid curiosity and
his histrionic moralizing.

"You will not, I know" he went on "mistake the very
deep nature of the grief that I feel—thoughts that do
often lie deep for tears" and whatever might seem defi-
cient in the quotation was amply compensated by the
nobility of his handsome head with its mane of white
hair as he uttered it "when I say that it is with his dear
ones—poor Mrs. Craddock, that boy and that girl,
that my thoughts lie so closely to-day. The last days,
I believe were most harrowing. Great pain and an all
too lively consciousness" he spoke with relish. "Our
poor friend, I fear, must have been oppressed by the
thought of the circumstances in which he would be
leaving those he loved. He had all that generous im-
providence which we proverbially associate with the
world of art which he so loved" he allowed his listeners
a slight twinkle of the eye at this mention of the childlike
nature of artists, but there was bitterness in the tone
of his voice as he recalled the disadvantageous light in
which his late colleague's generosity had placed his own
innate meanness.

"I am not personally acquainted with the family,
yet it would give me great pleasure to do all that I can
to assist them," and only by the twist of his smile did
he allow his scepticism of such a possibility to appear.

"That's very good of you, Earley" said Mr. Brunton.
"I may say now that I have certain schemes in mind and
I shall not hesitate to call upon your generous promise."

Dr. Earley's Adam's Apple wobbled slightly above

the points of the Gladstone collar with which, with morning coat and striped trousers, he habitually clothed the dignity of his old-world charm.

"But of course, my dear friend" he said hurriedly "I do beg also that you will not trouble yourself about the question of the Art Section of our little work." It was characteristic of him that where the others habitually spoke of their task as great he somehow magnified it by referring to it as little. "Poor Craddock naturally confided in me so many of his ideas, indeed our paths so constantly crossed. The Sister Muses, you know, have an unfortunate habit of refusing to be divided so conveniently as we could wish, they are really quite Siamese twins, so that I feel no hesitation in saying that I can safely offer. . . ."

But his offer was lost in the deep bellow of Mr. Cobbell's roar, as like a great Johnsonian lion he descended upon them, his huge chest covered by a double-breasted morning waistcoat across which his single eyeglass fluttered on its black silk ribbon like Beau Brummel's quiz.

"The late duke, of course" he was saying "resembled an ostler both in language and appearance, whilst there was, I remember, an ostler at 'Hutchings' who was curiously like the late duke's father." It was a remark which had always drawn applause from the American audiences of his ten-minute lectures on "England's Great Families". Dr. Noreen Maxwell gave him one of her Mona Lisa smiles. With her watery eyes, thin, wriggling body and mysterious smiles she seemed like an enigmatic eel.

"Mr. Brunton" she said, taking her chief's hand "we feel a great loss, but then we expected to, yes, in these last months we expected to." No one asked her what she meant, for intuition and prophecy were her feminine contributions to the circle, even in her historical work she was understood to feel and to apprehend rather than to know. "His work had gone as far as it could. Poor Mr. Craddock, he was beginning to look so puzzled. Men" she said, turning to Miss Wells "are awful babies really. They go on fitting the bricks together and then when one of them doesn't go into place they just can't make it out. I suppose" she said with a laugh "that's why God saw fit to make the illogical sex. We expect things to be a bit of a mystery and sometimes when one's dealing with the big things in life that's rather a help," and once again she smiled a little pityingly. Now, at any rate, her listeners felt they knew the direction in which her thoughts were moving and Mr. Cobbell hurried in with *his* claim to the vacant position.

"Poor Craddock" he roared "I'm afraid his difficulty was a very *practical* one. He'd exhausted the public galleries and he simply couldn't get to see the private collections. Our great families, you know, have their funny little ways, they need humouring. Simborough, for example, apparently refused to let him see his Tintoretto. Of course if I'd known I could have dealt with it straight-away. Dear old Simborough, all you've got to do is to praise his shorthorns."

The practical claims of the genealogist to take over the realm of art could not be set out more clearly. Any direct opposition that they might have met, however, was forgotten in the shock produced by the chief's next words.

"I had not intended to mention my ideas before our next weekly meeting" said Mr. Brunton. "I'd not really thought that the question of Craddock's successor would come up so soon", and he looked first at the white tombstones around them and then at his staff, "but I had forgotten your constant concern for the success of our enterprise. I am glad to say that I have thought of a scheme which, if we can put it into practice, will kill two birds with one stone. Craddock, who, by the way, seems to have been more generous with his confidences than I, at any rate, would ever have guessed, has talked to me a number of times in the last months about all the help his girl has been giving him. In fact I strongly suspect that a good number of the contributions that came in from him since last autumn were really her work, and if I'm right she not only knows what to say but also how to put it on paper. It's struck me that we could do ourselves and her a good turn by giving her the job. What do you think, Earley, do you think you could use her?"

If Mr. Brunton had calculated that the suddenness of his proposal would carry the day he had reckoned without the evasive determination that lay beneath his assistant's buttery manner. Dr. Earley had no intention of committing himself.

"It's a lovely proposal," he said, "a lovely proposal," and he stood for a moment in reverence before the beauty of it, "and just what I would have expected from you. What a wonderful chance for an untried girl—

to step straight into the shoes of a tried scholar, and of course, a princely salary for someone of her age." He glanced quizzically at his chief.

"I naturally shouldn't pay the girl what Craddock got" said Mr. Brunton, meeting his thrust with a direct riposte.

"I see," said Dr. Earley "I see," and by their looks the other scholars made it clear that they saw also. With such ammunition in their possession, and Mr. Brunton aware that they held it, they could afford to postpone the fight. Mr. Cobbell even felt able to venture upon Dr. Earley's preserve of trite quotations.

"The wind bites shrewdly" he bellowed "it is bitter cold. Will Shakespeare always has the last word. I shall be getting what old Brakehampton always called the rheumatises, extraordinary how the dialects persist in some old families. The present duchess, you know, always speaks of lilocks for lilac."

"Yes, indeed" said Dr. Noreen "il fait un froid de loup."

"One moment before we break up" said Mr. Brunton, ready now with the next thrust, "the difference between the girl's salary and her father's I thought of paying to young Craddock. Of course he'd have to give us a hand with the work, but it'll keep him going until his call-up. I don't know what he's good for, but apparently he's interested in the theatre, so he might give you a hand with some of the literary articles, Earley. It might also prove possible to relieve Miss Wells of some of her burden by getting *Mrs.* Craddock in now and again."

Poor Miss Wells looked quite shrivelled and once again her necklaces jangled. It was not so much the inroad on her salary, meagre though it was, that she feared, but rather any interference in the work which she regarded as so sacred a trust.

As Mr. Brunton moved off to his waiting Daimler the little group stood in bitter silence.

"Well" said Dr. Earley at last, "we have much food for thought from to-day's sad proceedings. Suppose we all assemble for tea before the meeting next week, at the A.B.C. shall we say?"

"The funeral baked meats" began Mr. Cobbell and then paused, somehow the quotation seemed to be in poor taste, and to venture twice on the Tom Tiddler's ground of Dr. Earley's preserves would be courting disaster.

"Good-bye, Dr. Earley" said Dr. Noreen taking his hand, "I have a most unwelcome guest awaiting me at home, one master Nicolo Machiavel", she was always on easy terms with the great, "he has such an unpleasant habit of putting poison in one's tea." She paused, then smiling enigmatically she threw her last bolt of woman's intuition, "I had such a strange feeling when Dr. Brunton was speaking that he meant something quite different to what his words implied," she said and was gone.

In a few seconds they had scattered to the four winds, to those sombre late Victorian homes in which high tea or supper awaited them. If only some Georgian poet could have saluted them as they departed "for Highgate and Highbury, Barnet and Ealing, for Richmond and Roehampton, Purley and Cheam."

It was really quite a neat little scheme that they devised at the tea-table, so much so that the ten minutes left to them before the meeting were passed in festive mood. Miss Wells, who was inclined to rich living, ordered a second Ovaltine; Dr. Earley sipped at his cold milk almost playfully; in a company of dyspeptics he alone had the distinction of a fully developed stomach ulcer. Mr. Cobbell became quite Horatian in mood as he discussed the Chablis at the last dinner of the "Friends of Old Books."

"When the secretary asked me what I thought of it" he boomed "I replied that it was certainly water stained, but that I doubted if it would leave me even *slightly* foxed."

Dr. Earley pinched Miss Well's leg and made a joke about "half calf."

"My wicked Caesar" said Dr. Noreen of her cat "killed my favourite little sparrow last night, and he wasn't a bit ashamed even when I told him that I should call him Caesar Borgia in future."

"Passer puellae meae mortuus est" bellowed Mr. Cobbell, and he looked almost lasciviously at Dr. Noreen as he added "Passer *deliciae* meae pullae."

"How lyrical, how musical they are!" cried Dr. Earley "Catullus and Tibullus. Only the Carolines I think ever caught the mood again exactly, and Austin Dobson" he added, "Austin Dobson, what a master of belles lettres! Austin Dobson, Garnett, Gosse, no one reads them now my girls tell me." He frequently made reference to his daughters in this way, sometimes even speaking of them as his girlies and always in so arch a manner that one might have fancied him master of a seraglio.

By the time they departed for the meeting the fun had reached a high pitch, everyone was talking at once. Through a maze of quotations given verbatim by Dr. Earley from his somewhat ambiguously titled reference book "Who did what to whom and where" Miss Wells could distinguish Dr. Noreen's report of an imaginary conversation held by her with "Kit" Marlowe in which she had whimsically indulged one evening the week before. Mr. Cobbell meanwhile was telling an amusing story of an American's encounter with the Earl of Crudeleigh, the realism of which must have been doubtful when he first heard it in 1921, and in which the American said to the Earl "Say bo" and referred to York Cathedral as a "Godbox." It was, Miss Wells felt, a real intellectual treat.

They were somewhat late at the encyclopaedia offices, where Mr. Brunton was already in impatient mood.

"We shall be able to have only the shortest possible discussion" he said "because I've invited Mrs. Craddock here to talk over any plans 'we may have made for her and her children. I hope you've decided upon the best means of rearranging the work to fit the new circumstances, Earley."

"My dear friend," and Dr. Earley's smile seemed to be all ill-fitting dentures, "if what we have to say should seem to hurt you, and I fear it will, for it hits at what you hold most dear—your charitable, your deeply charitable nature—remember that it is because we feel for once that your kindness, your too great sentiment, is in danger of sacrificing that standard of accuracy and scholarship which must always be our *first* concern. In entrusting the work of the encyclopaedia to untried, I would almost say, unknown hands you are allowing yourself an indulgence against which it is our duty to warn you."

"I find it difficult, Earley, to understand quite what you mean. If I remember rightly you were the *first* to urge our duty to the living, as I think you called it."

"And that duty must not be tied by any conditions" said Dr. Earley "which may make the gift turn sour in the mouths of giver and receiver alike. My dear old friend, indulge your generous impulses, it is your right, your nature, but let this be quite independent of our great work. A pension to the widow, for example, would surely fit the case. We, on our side, have decided to make a little collection among ourselves. It cannot of course be given the importance of what may come from you as poor Craddock's employer, his patron and confidant, but a simple tribute to the memory of a respected colleague." They had in fact computed the Danegeld most carefully.

Mr. Brunton was, for the moment, checked. He was not a wholly unkind man, but he was certainly not generous. He never believed in giving something for nothing, particularly since he felt certain that in securing Miss Craddock's services he would be getting a bargain. For a moment he sat silent. Then he said very decisively:

"I'm sorry I cannot agree. I think it only right in view of Craddock's opinion of his girl that she should be given a trial. As to the idea of a little monetary gift" he added smiling "I think it excellent, so long as it is offered with due respect for Mrs. Craddock's feelings. Nor can I think of your separating yourselves from me in this way. In the work of the encyclopaedia we are all colleagues." He paused for a moment whilst he reached a figure which would be an adequate embarrassment to them, then, "Indeed I will start by putting myself down for fifty pounds," he said.

Consternation was plain in every face, but any remonstrance was drowned by the loud grinding of a taxi's brakes as it drew up outside the windows. From this taxi, to their amazement, stepped Mrs. Craddock. It was a curious mode of transport for a suppliant woman.

Her appearance as she entered the room was even more amazing. They had none of them seen their colleague's wife except at the funeral, when their egocentric visions had painted in a conventional grief-stricken figure at the graveside, a stout, ageing female of no particular importance. Not that Mrs. Craddock would have claimed any importance for herself, she was the most modest of women, but she was decidedly not of the encyclopaedists' world. Large she was, but of the stoutness of a Rubens Venus or of the Wife of Bath, with purple hair and plenty of make-up. If she had been shy they might have found it easier, but though she clearly felt unfamiliar, it was not in her nature to be other than "at home," and as soon as the introductions were complete, she began to talk.

"It's very kind of you to let me come and see where Hugh worked, Mr. Brunton," and what with her common accent and her flashy clothes Miss Wells was hard put to

it to know what to think. "Oh yes, and thank you all
for coming to the funeral," she added, "I'm afraid I
didn't shake hands or anything as I should, but I always
get upset when I'm meant to be dignified." She was so
short of breath when she spoke that Dr. Noreen Maxwell
decided that she drank.

"It was a sad occasion for all of us" said Mr. Brunton
hesitatingly, for even he was rather put out. "I asked
you here, Mrs. Craddock, because in association with
your husband's colleagues I wanted to make you an
offer of help. I know how suddenly poor Craddock's
death came and I felt that perhaps with the two children
to provide for, of whom, by the way, he always spoke
to me so warmly, you might be somewhat difficultly
placed."

"Nothing" said Mrs. Craddock "except the house.
Poor old Hugh, always meant to put aside, of course,
but what with Vera always winning scholarships and
Ronnie never winning them, we've spent a fortune on
their education. But the house is mine, I'm glad to
say, Hugh saw to that." She smiled rather broadly,
and Mr. Cobbell recognized to his surprise what in
another sphere he had come to regard as the manner
of a gracious lady. "Luckily I've got a bit in the post
office that'll carry us through for a month or so, but it's
very kind of you to think of it."

"As to money" said Mr. Brunton "Craddock's
colleagues and I will be deeply hurt if you will not
accept a small sum we have collected to show our
appreciation of all that he has done for the encyclopaedia. I hope to be able to present you with a little

cheque for £100, am I right, Earley?" he asked maliciously, and Dr. Earley said hurriedly.

"About that, yes."

"Well I'm certainly not going to refuse. Whatever I might do for myself, I couldn't possibly where the children are concerned. I'm glad you appreciated Hugh, he certainly took a lot of trouble over the work. And thank you very much."

"I didn't do that very well, I'm afraid" she said confidentially to Dr. Noreen "but then I'm a bit nervous."

All Dr. Noreen's powers of enigmatic speech had vanished before Mrs. Craddock's buoyancy, so she twisted her face into what she felt to be a more than usually Mona Lisa smile, and succeeded somewhat unhappily in recalling to the widow the effects of Mr. Craddock's last paralytic stroke.

"What I chiefly had in mind, though" continued Mr. Brunton "was the idea that your daughter, who I know from your husband's account, and from some of her writing that I've seen, is a most promising scholar, should take on her father's work on the encyclopaedia. Part of it at first, perhaps, later possibly all."

"Well that is good of you" said Mrs. Craddock, "but I don't somehow think that's what Vera's got in mind. It would mean refusing her scholarship and that wouldn't be right, would it? You see," she said in confident explanation to Dr. Earley, "really good qualifications are so important in scholarly work to-day. That was what held Hugh back really," she smiled happily at Mr. Brunton. "Thank you very much, though" she said "that was really a very kind thought and I can see it would be ever such fun for her working with you all," here she looked particularly at Miss Well's emaciated features, "and I'll ask her, of course, but I think she'll say no."

"And how about your boy, Mrs. Craddock?" asked Dr. Earley. He could guess at the effect upon their chief of Mrs. Craddock's simple rejection of his well-laid schemes to secure a bargain, and he derived considerable pleasure in pursuing the matter. "After all, the men of the land still deserve some attention as I tell my girlies. It'll be a trying time for him hanging about waiting to do his military service, to which no doubt he's looking forward like most of the young fellows."

"Well, as to that I'm surprised to hear it" said Mrs. Craddock. "But I expect you know best. Anyhow, Ronnie isn't, I'm afraid. Not of course that he doesn't want to do what he should, but he certainly isn't looking forward to it. He talks about getting some extra work at the studios while he's hanging about. He's stage mad, you know."

"Ah, yes!" said Dr. Earley "so I heard. Mr. Brunton was thinking he might like to give me a hand with the drama section."

"Oh, dear" said Mrs. Craddock "I shouldn't think that would do at all. Ronnie's very gay, you know" she added, winking at Dr. Noreen Maxwell. "No, I'm afraid, you might as well ask me."

"And how," asked Mr. Cobbell, of all the party his social conceptions were most outraged, "and how do you propose to maintain these two young people?"

"Well," said Mrs. Craddock "to be honest with you I'm going to let the whole house out in lodgings. It's a large house and I'm used to students' ways and there's quite a lot of money to be made that way these days and still do a good part by them."

"I see" said Dr. Earley "a good part" and he repeated the expression once or twice. It was not a concept with which he felt familiar.

Surprise and anger had prevented Mr. Brunton from speaking for some minutes. The more kindly genial side of his nature, which he reserved for his private life and particularly for his academic hobby, was not proof against the rush of more brutal sentiments which surged up in him as he saw his offer rejected in this offhand manner by a person of absolutely no importance. To lose his bargain through the obstinacy of a fool, to have his patronage overlooked by a subordinate choked him with rage, and that this subordinate and fool should be a woman roused all the misogynistic fears that lay beneath his valeted bachelor existence.

"I only hope, Mrs. Craddock" he said with an icy fury "that you will organize the rest of your children's future with the same frivolous obstinacy that you have shown here this afternoon. If so, you should have the pleasure of seeing them in the bread line before you have finished. Should that eventuality arise" he continued, "and I hardly see how it can be avoided, please remember that no assistance whatever will be forthcoming from me."

If the others had sensed the storm in the air Mrs. Craddock was quite overwhelmed with astonishment when it broke upon her. For a moment her lips trembled, and then she spoke rather quietly.

"I'm afraid I must have said the wrong thing. It's not easy to say what one means, is it?" she asked turning to Dr. Noreen, but it was clear that this was not Dr. Noreen's experience, so Mrs. Craddock went on hurriedly "I tried to say how grateful I was and so I'm sure Ronnie and Vera will be. Maybe Vera will think differently, I'll certainly ask her."

"There will be no need" Mr. Brunton replied, for by now his fury had overruled his self-interest. "The offer is withdrawn. I should not wish anyone to work upon the encyclopaedia who thought so poorly of it. You don't perhaps know that during these last months we were carrying your husband as a passenger, otherwise perhaps you would show us a little more gratitude."

But Mrs. Craddock's lips were no longer trembling, she was staring up at Mr. Brunton in disgust.

"Well, of all the mean things" she said, "now I know why Hugh looked so low sometimes." She was about to add something more sharp, when she cried out "Oh! Lord what's the good?" and gathering her handbag to her she went quickly out of the room, leaving behind her a trail of Californian Poppy.

Mr. Brunton sat hunched over the table for a moment. No one dared to speak. Then he lifted his head; raising one eyebrow quizzically, he looked sharply at his staff with his little beady eyes.

"It'll take a good deal of hard work to get the taste of that out of our mouths" he said, and left them.

Though, in fact, they had won the day, though the

encyclopaedia remained uncontaminated and Mr. Craddock's job still open to competition, they yet shared
their chief's anger and disgust. That she should have
taken the money and refused the advice, it was more
than Miss Wells could have believed possible. Dr.
Noreen asked if they had not noticed something peculiar
about the woman's eyes? No? Well, if they hadn't, no
matter; it was probably one of those things that only a
woman would see. Mr. Cobbell remembered Lady
Breconwood telling him of just such a case of ingratitude
from a housekeeper in the old Viscount's day. But
Dr. Earley was at heart more realistic, or perhaps his
belief in himself was more securely grounded. He saw
only that they had secured their point. He preferred
to take a more kindly view.

"She was not, I hasten to confirm it," he said, "one
of our world. That much is certain. But I think I
detected some change, some softening of her manner,
suggesting that even on that stony ground learning's
little tribute had not fallen quite fruitlessly."

Sister Superior

SHE had intended Claire to find her seated, idle and cool, in her deck-chair on the lawn, ready to dawdle through the first day of the visit in a leisurely, gracious manner, and now, before she had finished arranging the gladioli in the hall, she could hear the wheels of the car crushing the gravel on the drive. She looked with dismay at the muddle of broken stalks, discarded pink flower heads and sodden newspaper on the oval table. So often this summer she and Gillian had got through all their housework well before eleven and had been able to lie on the beach in the sun—their Boots library books no more than excuses—or to sit quietly on the porch in happy neglect of the piles of Robert's unmended socks beside them; but to-day they must, of course, get behindhand with everything, despite their omission of the usual second cigarette over the breakfast table debris. It was largely, of course, stage nerves. Not even twenty years of happy marriage, motherhood, widowhood, could erase her timid worship, her awkward reverence before Claire's sophistication and charm. She found herself feeling for the slipping petticoat, the falling hairslide; and on looking in the mirror, a patch of red, peeling sunburnt skin on the temple and a wisp of greying sun-bleached hair fallen untidily across her eye, seemed to put her once more into that shapeless gym frock and those wrinkled black cotton stockings —she was back at once in their bedroom at Paignton tidying the confusion of frocks and make-up that her sister's whirlwind movements left behind her, hearing her quick chatter on the terrace below and the answering laughter of an admiring group of their father's "snotties." But memory changed to reality without a break as she heard Claire getting out of the car, the same note of excitement and conscious charm in her voice, unchanged over all the years. Flustered and anxious, she ran to greet her on the steps.

"Mary, darling" called Claire and she swallowed the hot, dumpy little figure in a close embrace, then, still grasping her shoulders, she held her at arm's length and examined her with quizzical, but affectionate regard.

"Mary, it's disgusting, you've put on fat" she said, and turning to her niece "How does she?" she asked, all mock wonderment, "how does she contrive to wax so fat, when all the rest of the world is starving?"

"It can't be the amount Mummy eats or from sitting still" said Gillian; her reply was mumbled, hardly audible. She resented her aunt greatly and her own shyness even more. "She never gives herself a moment's rest."

Claire gave the assumed smile she reserved for all imperfectly heard remarks of younger people.

"Not that you probably seem out of place down here, Mary dear" she laughed, "for I've *never, never* seen such enormous people as got into the train at Didcot. One terrible, blowsy old woman, my dear, who overflowed on top of me, with terrible beery breath and a great fat face with a white whiskery chin, just like Aunt Evelyn."

"Oh, Claire, really,!" protested Mary, "Aunt Evelyn never had beery breath."

"Now darling, don't start standing up for all those old dead and buried horrors. Your great Aunt Evelyn" she continued turning to Gillian "was a dreadful old church-going creature who made everybody's life a misery who would let her—and that means you, Mary—and who ought to have died years before she did. Yes, she should have done, Mary,—trying to stop you from marrying just so that she could have someone to play Racing Demon with."

Mary laughed happily, she always felt so deeply grateful when her sister even implied praise of her. "You must be exhausted, Claire" she said, and then felt ashamed to have suggested any imperfection in so graceful, erect a figure, with her soft skin and deep grey eyes, still so lovely for all her fifty years.

"I *have* had rather a ghastly time with the shop recently" Claire replied. "Doctor Redman's just the tiniest bit worried about my overworking and not sleeping" but, satisfied by her sister's look of alarm, "We're not going to spoil this heavenly holiday you're giving me by talking about that" she said.

"Oh, Claire, *I* giving you a holiday?" said Mary in a solemn, embarrassed voice, "you mustn't talk like that." She always felt a burning shame when she contrasted Claire's life with her own, as though the whole natural order of justice had been overthrown. The failure of Claire's marriage—those terrible women and the sordid horror of the divorce court—her rootless existence as she moved from one small hotel to another, her plucky attempt to make ends meet with the shop—made her own happy life seem somehow disgraceful and the little financial help she gave Claire from time to time an agony of shame and presumption to her.

"Why we've been talking of nothing else but your visit for weeks, haven't we, Gillian," she cried.

Even Gillian felt ashamed of her annoyance at Claire's smart lime linen dress with its padded hips and three-quarter length skirt that made herself and her mother look so dowdy; after all, Aunt Claire was so gay and brave in face of all the troubles she had.

"Mother and Robert have done nothing but make plans for weeks" she said.

"And you, Gillian?" asked Claire; she could not endure dissent.

"Oh, don't expect Gillian to talk about herself" said Mary. "Happiness always ties her tongue into knots."

"Which it never did with you, Mary, of course" said Claire laughing, and then impulsively, regally, she kissed them both in turn. "Oh! you darlings" she said.

Claire sat on her bed, smoking a cigarette, whilst her sister unpacked her cases and put away her clothes—it was quite like old times.

"Roses in my bedroom" she said, "Mary, darling, you mustn't spoil me. You forget that I'm not terribly used to attention these days."

"Claire, dear" said Mary, laying down a pair of out-door shoes on the dressing table and standing quite still, "Why don't you give it all up and come down here?"

Claire stretched full length on the bed and blew smoke into the air, it might have to come to that later, but so long as she could keep going on subsidies she could afford to be realistic.

"Mary!" she laughed "darling! you never change, always so sentimental. Why, we'd have murdered each other within a month." Then abruptly she asked "How's Robert?"

"Oh he's awfully well" said Mary, "he had to go up to Oxford for his viva to-day, but he's rushing back to see you to-morrow. His tutor thinks he ought to have done very well. We hardly dare to hope for a first, but. . . ."

Claire got up and began to pencil in her mouth.

"Oh, yes, of course" she said in little jerks as she shaped her lips to the stick "the examinations. But girls, Mary, isn't he in love yet?"

"I don't think there's anyone in particular" said Mary "he's been very busy of course."

Claire swung round, laughing, "Anyone in particular! Really, Mary dear, you're talking like Mother. I should hope not indeed, why he ought to be breaking every heart in the neighbourhood," and then as Mary smiled, she said very slowly "You're not holding him, are you Mary dear?"

"Holding?"

"Yes, darling, it's a little habit mothers have and it never works out well."

"I really don't think I'm possessive. Why! this vacation he's hardly been at home at all."

Claire sat down before the dressing table mirror and

began to clean her nails with an orangewood stick, she looked carefully at her sister's reflection busily folding a blouse.

"And you don't like it, Mary, that's it, isn't it?" she asked.

Mary reflected anxiously, her conscience was easily troubled.

"We miss him, of course, it's a bit dull for Gillian."

"Oh! Gillian!" said Claire.

Mary was immediately on the defensive. "What do you mean? Gillian and Robert are very fond of one another that's all."

"Mary dear, I think that's faintly improper, at least from anyone but you it would be. Gillian's only seventeen you know, no young man wants to spend his days with his baby sister."

"Oh, I know" said Mary, "but Gillian's the last person to get in anyone's way, she's tremendously independent."

"She's tremendously *pretty*" said Claire.

Her sister coloured with pleasure. "Oh, do you think so? Do tell her, Claire, please. She gets far too few compliments."

"I'm rather afraid" said Claire "that she gets far too little of lots of things. Her mouth's a very unhappy one."

Mary felt as though the ground was shaking beneath her, Gillian's lack of social life was a constant source of anxiety to her.

"Oh, I *do* hope not," she cried. "It's so difficult to tell with Gillian. We're such very good friends, but she never says much. I suppose," she added, "that she's too like me, afraid of sentiment."

Claire got up and put her arm round her sister's rather thick waist.

"I think perhaps, darling, I could help a certain amount with both of them," and she stroked her sister's hip. "They'll probably talk to me just because I don't matter all that much to them."

"Oh, they're very fond of you," cried Mary.

"I said 'all that much', " replied Claire. "Have I your permission to make myself just a little important to them?"

Mary laughed, she was slightly frightened of her sister in these moods. "That won't be very difficult," she said, and then she added more seriously, "You know how happy it would make me to know that they had you to go to with their problems."

Her senses were thrilled at this mysterious help that Claire would give to her children, but behind that her mind was troubled as to quite why help should be needed. She had thought everything was going so well, but Claire had such tremendous intuition, could see so much deeper.

"Have another one, Claire?" said Robert. "What shall it be, another pink gin?" and he picked up her glass from the little saloon bar table.

"A pink gin sounds delightful." Claire's tone was almost that of a young girl taken out for the first time, and yet Robert knew that he was entertaining a clever, sophisticated woman. He was on his mettle as a man of the world; thank God he knew the barman well.

"Two more pink gins, Jimmy," he called.

It was really a most exciting friendship to find in the midst of one's family where everything was normally so dull.

"It sounds as though she was out for what she could get," said Claire, as Robert sat down again, "but of course you could judge best about that."

"Oh," said her nephew carelessly, "I knew she was on the make, but . . ."

"But so were you," laughed the aunt, "and did you succeed?"

The boy's thin, pale face flushed slightly, he felt ashamed of the whole affair now, after all nothing had actually happened.

"Well, as a matter of fact, I thought it wiser not. A landlady's daughter, you know, and in Oxford itself."

"I know," smiled Claire, "you had to be careful." Then she shook his hand and said gravely, "Don't be too careful, Robert. Women can find it an awful bore. I'm saying all this, you know, because, well—your mother's the sweetest darling in the world, but she isn't really the person to understand quite what hell life can be when one's growing up. She was born old, you know, and then there was never anyone but your father. I wasn't quite like that," she smiled cynically and flicked the ash from her cigarette. "I went in for having what's called a good time," and she laughed bitterly.

Three pink gins made Robert feel the full force of this bitterness, woe to the man who had thrown a stone at his aunt at that moment! He pressed her hand.

"No, Robert," she said, "no. You mustn't be silly. I'm

old enough, well . . . old enough to be your aunt. The
good time was all right, it was just me that didn't know
how to take it. It wasn't really quite my fault, your grand-
parents never told us anything, you see. That's what
made Mary, bless her, such a babe in arms."

"Yes," laughed Robert, "Mother's an incredible
innocent. I couldn't possibly tell her half of what I've
told you this morning."

"I should hope not," replied Claire. "Confidence in
parents—yes, but confidences, never, never."

Behind the artificial worldliness that drink provided,
Robert felt a twinge of disloyalty.

"Mother and Gillian are far too good to me," he said.

"*Far* too good," echoed Claire. "That's the trouble
with strong affections, my dear, they impose such a duty
on one. You'll have to fight damned hard, you know,
to stop them sacrificing themselves, but you must do it
Robert, for your own sake and their's."

Robert's face was gravity itself.

"I know," he said solemnly. It was most extraordinary to find oneself in so dramatic a situation.

"It's an old story," said Claire, and her nephew
nodded his head wisely. "Sometimes it's useful to have
a friend who isn't quite so blind, so let me know when I
can help. Is it a bargain?" and she held out her small,
well-manicured hand. Robert took it in his own. The
compact, he felt, was clean, modern, sensible. There was
no doubt Claire was a real good scout. Claire put her
cigarette case and lighter in her handbag.

"I mustn't be late for Mary's famous picnic. She is the
most wonderful child in her ideas of entertainment."

"I know," said Robert tolerantly, "I can't say it's exactly what I'd have chosen for an afternoon's gaiety."

"But good heavens! Robert *you're* not coming with all those tabbies and small children."

"Mother expects me to. I always have, you know. Didn't you hear her this morning?"

"I couldn't have been listening," Claire laughed. "Well it's your own choice," she said, but she looked quite grave.

"Don't you think I ought to?" asked Robert.

"My dear Robert, you're twenty-one, and I hope, of sound mind . . . *I* can't say what you ought to do."

"But do you think it's silly," urged her nephew.

"I think it's fantastic," she replied.

Gillian walked very slowly along the promenade, being very careful to tread only on the lines of the pavement; she felt some satisfaction to her nerves from the noise that her mackintosh made against the ground as she purposefully dragged it behind her. The whole afternoon had been a fiasco—the rain, the boring old women, the tired, fractious children, the tide wrong for bathing, her mother's inability to cope. She had not realized how much she would miss Robert's support on the annual outing, if it hadn't been for Aunt Claire's energy she dreaded to think what depths of failure they might have plumbed. At the last she had taken refuge in giggling at Aunt Claire's caustic asides. It was this above all that had made her so angry; it was bad enough that Robert should fall under the influence of their aunt's cheap

charm, but that *she* should be disloyal to her mother in
this way had added the weight of guilt to the already
deep burden of resentment and boredom. As they
dropped the children and the old women one by one at
their front doors a mood of brooding sulkiness had begun
to close in upon her such as she had not known since
childhood, shutting out the external world with a fog of
self-pity, urging her to assert herself, to show that she
too had a right to rebellion, could not always be counted
on to be dutiful and correct in her behaviour. She had
purposely lagged behind her mother and aunt, telling
herself that she must avoid a row, yet half-hoping that
her ostentatious withdrawal would call forth comment.
It was so completely selfish, she thought, of Robert to
back out like that at the last minute—everyone knew
that the picnic was a nuisance, but it gave Mother great
pleasure and it only happened once a year, they had
always managed to get fun out of it before. Mother had
accepted Robert's defection so easily too.

"Gillian won't mind being nursemaid on her own for
one afternoon."

And Aunt Claire, "Perhaps, Mary dear, it isn't exactly
the occasion for a young man who's president of his
college J.C.R. You did say J.C.R. didn't you, Robert?"

As though the difference between seventeen and twenty
was a lifetime.

"Gillian," called Mary, "we ought to hurry, dear. If
we're going to listen to that play we shall have to rush
with supper a bit."

Gillian's mackintosh was almost scraped to pieces as
she approached them.

"Darling, your mackintosh!" said Mary. Gillian appeared to take no notice. "Mrs. Truefitt says Horniman's have got some grapefruit in," said Mary, "do you like grapefruit, Claire?"

"Yes, Mary, I love them," replied her sister.

"Gillian's very fond of them, aren't you, darling?" went on Mary.

"Does it matter much *what* I like?" said Gillian savagely.

"Why Gillian, darling. . . ." Mary was lost in bewilderment, but before she could say more Gillian had begun to run wildly away from them towards the house. "Whatever is the matter?" called her mother.

Claire put her hand on her arm. "It's been a very tiring afternoon, Mary," she said.

"But I can't understand it. Gillian's never like this. Oh dear! I'm afraid the picnic wasn't a very great success."

"It went very well, Mary," said her sister soothingly. "Don't you see, dear, Gillian's bound to be a little overwrought at times, it's a difficult age for a girl, neither one thing nor the other," and as Mary stared uncomprehendingly, "let me have a little talk with her," she added.

As Claire entered the kitchen, Gillian was assembling the crockery for the evening meal with a clatter that would have announced her anger to a party of the blind.

"I don't want any help, thank you," she shouted.

"And I've no intention of giving any," said Claire.

"Then perhaps you'll keep out of the way. You've made enough trouble already."

"Gillian, my dear, don't be so melodramatic," said her aunt, "that's what I hate about you self-sacrificing people. It's entirely your own fault, you know. You've got more brains and push than Robert any day, but you prefer to sit back and watch your mother spoiling him and feel yourself unappreciated and misunderstood."

"I haven't exactly noticed you discouraging Robert from being selfish," said her niece.

"My dear, if I've spent a lot of time with your brother, that's because I'm not a fool and I know where I'm not wanted. Besides, you see, dear, I like to be with people who are alive and getting what they want out of life."

Going up to the girl, she put her hand on her shoulder. "You've got everything, my dear, if you liked to use it—the brains, the looks, the sense of humour, but instead of that you prefer to be a taciturn, faithful hound to the family, and it makes you a bore to everyone, yourself included."

Gillian's overwrought nerves broke into sobbing and she clutched her aunt hysterically.

"It isn't fair," she said, "it isn't fair."

"I know," said Claire, "not to you or Robert or your mother. You've just got to stop being a doormat."

Then drawing Gillian on to a kitchen chair, she sat with her arm round the girl's waist. "Let's talk about it a little, shall we?" she said, "I think we ought to be able to evolve a plan. . . ."

Mary folded Claire's dresses one by one and put them in the suitcases, while her sister lay back on the bed. It was quite like old times, when she used to pack for Claire to go to stay with the Chudleigh's or Admiral Kemp at Clifton. She did not know how she was going to manage when her sister had gone, Robert and Gillian were proving so difficult, and Claire understood the whole thing so well, indeed had sensed the problem long before she, their own mother, was aware of it.

"I *do* wish you didn't have to go, dear," she said, "you've helped the children so much since you've been here. I'm afraid it hasn't been very amusing with all these quarrels. I can't think what's come over them both, but I expect you're right and it's all been going on for a long time, only I just haven't noticed it."

"Darling Mary," smiled Claire, "you were never made for troubled waters, were you? You see, darling, youth's a very selfish thing, and unless one takes great care one gets imposed on."

"Perhaps I've expected too much from them," said Mary anxiously, "I've never meant to stand in their way."

"And you don't, darling. All this business about youth having its own life to lead is all very well, but you've got yours too, don't forget that. Oh! I do hope you'll manage. Thank God I've been able to be of some use while I was down here."

"You've done everything," said Mary.

Claire shook her head, and then lay back upon the bed sighing.

"Oh dear! I'm not looking forward to returning to the shop," she said. "Miss Cameron's letter to-day wasn't exactly encouraging. She means well, but heaven knows what sort of a mess she's got into, and things weren't easy when I left."

"Claire, darling," said Mary, "how selfish we've been bothering you with all our troubles, when you have so many of your own. Tell me all about it, please."

Claire smiled cynically. "It's not very original, my dear," she said, "just the usual thing. The bank difficult, wholesaler's bills unpaid, not much coming in. People just don't seem to want hand-made brooches."

"Claire," said Mary, and she looked away in embarrassment. "I've wanted so much to ask you to let me help you. I got £70 the other day from that tea company Daniel bought shares in, please let me give it to you."

Claire's face, as she looked up, was for a moment really angry with disappointment, she smiled shyly.

"It's sweet of you, darling. I wish that was all there was to it. £70 would only be a drop in the ocean."

"Oh! my dear," said Mary, "have things been so bad and you never told me. It was naughty of you. Claire, please, darling, will you send all these wretched bills to me and let me settle them," and as Claire made a gesture of protest, she added, "please, darling. It's such a very little I can do to repay you for all you've done down here for me and the children."

Such Darling Dodos

"I THINK it vastly disobliging in you, cousin" said Tony, "to be at so much pains over me."

It was thirty years ago now since he had first adopted this imitation Jane Austen speech in addressing the academical branch of his family; it represented the furthest concession he felt prepared to make to the whimsical humour of North Oxford.

"I've brought you *The Times*," said Priscilla, "I hope that was right."

She was not expected to reply in the same jargon. She drew the curtains apart, letting the sunlight fall full upon her visitor as he sat up in bed. It was all that Tony could do not to scream: to be seen by anyone but Mrs. Fawcett before he had made his morning toilet was monstrous enough, to be revealed in every line and wrinkle was an outrage. Thus floodlit, he did indeed look far older than his fifty-five years, his long thin Greco features chalk white against the crimson eiderdown, his nose, chin and cheekbones all highlights where the sun shone upon the greasy cold cream, the artifice of the black waved hair too clearly revealed beneath the neat mesh of the slumber net. He looked with distaste at the bowl of puffed wheat and anticipated with dread the inevitable strong Indian tea.

"Is it all right?" said Priscilla anxiously. She stood with her hands held awkwardly at her sides, rocking from one foot to another like a giant schoolgirl. Pathos

always made her feel awkward and anxious, and at
the moment she felt very deeply the pathos of this
lonely, ageing, snobbish old man whom she tolerated
only through childhood ties.   Pathos was Priscilla's
dominating sensation, it had led her into Swaraj and
Public Assistance Committees, into Basque Relief and
Child Psychiatry Clinics; at the moment it kept her on a
Rent Restriction Tribunal; it fixed her emotionally as a
child playing dolls' hospitals. Tony smoothed his eyebrows
with his fingers and looked at the breakfast tray; he decided to take the remark as referring to Priscilla's dress.

"*All right*, my dear?" he said "it's *quite* charming."
Priscilla was not surprised at the twist of the conversation, it was so much a family tradition that cousin Tony
should know about women's clothes and arranging
flowers. Mother had always referred to these accomplish-
ments with a smile, it had been her version of Father's
"nincompoop."   Later in the nineteen-twenties, after
she had married Robin, Priscilla herself had discussed
the whole problem with him in more Freudian terms;
but for the last twenty years, the family had been content to let the matter drop. The thought that for Tony
himself it must of course be still a living issue made her
feel weary beyond measure. She looked down for relief
at her blue linen dress with its long, full skirt.

"Robin hates these long skirts," she said.

"My dear Priscilla" said Tony, "I should have hoped
that, after more than twenty years of matrimony, you
would have ceased to believe that men know anything
whatsoever about their wive's clothes. I should think
a great deal less of dear Robin if he did take kindly to

changing fashion." Tony always put himself on the feminine side of the fence in this way.

"You don't think the colour wrong?" asked Priscilla.

Tony closed his eyes in despair "No, no, it's quite perfect" he said and reflected that, no matter how long or short, dresses on Priscilla would always seem like hand-woven djibbahs.

With his long, bony and blue-veined hands he spread out *The Times* in front of him. It was more than he could endure to face the leaders nowadays, they were so dreadfully socialistic. Only last week he had said to his friend Mildred Brough-Owen "I really believe that I should take the *Telegraph* if I wasn't so afraid of finding that I actually *knew* some of the curious people who announce their marriages in its columns. It would be too shaming."

"Let us see what fresh horror the Government have in store for us" he said and then remembered that it was not the comforting, motherly tones of Mrs. Fawcett that would reply to him. Christian charity and good manners, he reminded himself, must be observed, after all he was *in partibus infidelium*, the land of invincible ignorance, and he smiled to himself at his little Catholic joke.

"Ah" he went on quickly before Priscilla could protest, "this is surely the crowning horror of all. Violet Durrant's daughter is going to breed and they have the impudence to announce the fact in advance. Well we can't say we haven't been warned. Anything more unpleasant than *that* young woman with a big belly I cannot imagine."

He often spoke in this way, it was a coarse directness that he felt to be a mark of the grand seigneur. It made Priscilla feel most uncomfortable as though a curate had walked into the room naked but for his clerical collar, and yet, she reminded herself, she lived in a circle where frankness of speech was taken for granted. Tony was delighted at her embarrassment, it confirmed his cherished belief in the essentially middle-class narrowness of the university world, and, in particular, of his tiresome progressive relations.

He gazed with real distaste at Priscilla as she stood fingering the knob of the door. It was quite absurd that at over fifty she should not know what to say or when to go. With her enormous height and ample frame, her flaxen hair and bovine eyes, she was like a head prefect in the role of a Rhine maiden. Surely, he thought, there must be some delinquent child or unmarried mother to claim her attention even at this hour of the morning.

"You get more like Aunt Ethel every time I see you," he said acidly; remembering his aunt he could think of no more satisfactory insult. But Priscilla smiled happily.

"Do you think so, Tony?" she asked, "I should be glad of that. Mother was such a very self-sufficient person. Some people thought her callous after father died. She wasn't of course, she felt it very deeply, but her life was too full to allow time for mourning, and that sort of thing."

Too full of meddlesomeness, thought Tony, too little occupied with her duty as a mother. Maternity always wore a halo of sanctity for him.

"I doubt if we can any of us hope to be self-sufficient, Priscilla," he said, "I'm quite sure that we should be very unhappy if we were."

He had come here to help his cousin in her trouble and he was not going to be put off by sentimentality. Only his duty as a Catholic could have brought him to a house with such distasteful associations, it was something of this duty that he hoped to make clear to her.

"If Robin dies," Priscilla said, "I must be self-sufficient you know, Tony. I'm not going to hang round Nick all the time. I've seen too many mothers like that."

"I should hope not indeed," said Tony, "though Nick, I am sure, will know his duty. No, my dear, if it's only human ties you're thinking of, I'm afraid you *will* be alone, very much alone."

Priscilla frowned. "Oh, I see what you mean," she said, "It's very kind of you, Tony dear, but don't you think God's rather a habit? I don't think I could acquire new habits at fifty. I don't mean to be shocking," she added.

Tony was delighted, here was one of his favourite openings, he laughed gaily.

"Oh, Priscilla darling, how little all these years of high thinking have done to break down your Protestant conscience. No, my dear, there's far too much real evil in the world to allow time for being shocked at human folly. I'm afraid being shocked is one of the indulgences we Catholics can't afford" and then he added less sharply, "*Fifty* years' habit, did you say? Surely Priscilla, you can't be satisfied with a view of time which is, frankly my dear, so provincial?"

"Provincial isn't the kind of word that affects me, Tony," said Priscilla. "It's all *my* life. There won't be so much more time and I've been able to clear up so pitifully little of the muddle."

"Oh, my dear, if you're going to constitute yourself charwoman to the world," his voice rose to coloratural heights and he smiled with Mona Lisa wisdom.

But Priscilla smiled too. "I'm afraid I took that job on a long time ago" she said and went out of the room.

What with the over-harsh lighting and the dirty fly-blown glass of the dressing table mirror, placed, of course, exactly where it should not have been, it took Tony quite a long time to give his skin that smooth stretched appearance, his cheeks that discreetly rosy shade with which he was accustomed to face the world, and even then he suddenly noticed a great white daub of shaving cream under the lobe of his left ear. He felt quite agitated and depressed as he combed the black waves into place—the side bits were no sooner tinted than they seemed to need re-doing. He sat by the window for a little, filing his nails—they were so brittle nowadays, he felt sure it was something to do with this horrible food. The front garden was as neglected and melancholy now as when he had first known it at the turn of the century. When all the other gardens of the Woodstock Road were ablaze with laburnum and lilac and red may, "Courtwood" always wore this lugubrious aspect— "si triste, si morne" he always said in describing it. So often as a child he had sought relief from the oppression of the house among the dusty golden privet and the spotted laurel bushes, the lower branches of which seemed always hung with brown, dead leaves. He had sat so often on the mossy stones in the damp angles of the huge red brick Italianate house, among broken stones and pieces of china covered by snail tracks and spiders' webs, companioned only by toads. No doubt at this very moment a few solitary Solomon's Seal were in flower, to be followed later in the year by some pitiful straggling montbretia.

He turned from the window with a shudder. The Harkers had always been too busy to look after the house or the garden or the food; too busy, he reflected, covering reality over with reading and talking, too busy making things that were better not made and experimenting with things that should have been left alone, too busy urging rights and forgetting duties—a futile struggle to justify by works alone. And yet in their company it was *he* that always felt so very limited, so very uninteresting, so beside the point—absurdly, of course, because even before he came into the Church, he had been infinitely more sensitive, more "alive to people," and afterwards, well—one must always beware of spiritual pride.

All the same, even now he had only to enter "Courtwood's" gates to feel dull and irrelevant. He could walk up the Woodstock Road with the sensitive approach of dear Mrs. Dalloway or the humorous eye of beloved Lizzie Bennett, and yet once past those gates and his personality seemed to shrink, he would become aware of a curious, ridiculous sensation of having missed the essentials of life. He could only suppose that it was a hangover from childhood, when the great house and its occupants had loomed so large and solid above him, when his very protest against the lack of comfort and the ugliness had been made to seem petty and trivial. Safe in his bedroom he used to pour over Richard Le Gallienne or, hidden among the laurels, bathe himself in the beauty of Beardsley's *Volpone* or Dowson's poems; but there had always been a return at last to the underboiled blue mutton, to Uncle Stephen with his telepathic communications in Ancient Greek and his White Knight electrical experiments, to Aunt Ethel protesting at the conditions of Chinese forced labour. With ears full of Stravinsky and eyes full of Bakst, he had later to suffer with a widowed Aunt Ethel as, tears in her eyes, she cast down for ever the family Liberal gods and solemnly cursed Asquith and Grey for the outrage of Forcible Feeding.

Even when that dreadful guardianship was finally at an end, his visits though more rare, more independent, had been somehow, none the less humiliating. He had, for example, behaved so well during that absurd little scene in the 'thirties, and yet the memory of it was not exactly comfortable. He had entered that awful sitting-room with its Heal's furniture, its depressingly sensible typewriter and long low bookcases to be met by a phalanx of grey flannel trousered young men and bespectacled young women in cotton dresses busy with tea and leaflets and sandwiches for—of all enormities —these wretched, misguided hunger marchers. Robin had been bustling about among them in a butcher blue shirt and a red tie quite unsuitable to a man of his age with a mop of untidy white hair, and Priscilla presided like a Roman matron in a terrible arty check gingham dress and sandals; yet, caricatures though they looked, they had been familiar and happy with the younger generation in a way that had made him unaccountably envious. Of course that was the period of irresponsibility, not the gay irresponsibility of his own unregenerate days, but an awful gloomy irresponsibility which was far more dangerous, the period of that unfortunate "King and Country" motion with its serious consequences abroad. He had spoken most sharply to Robin—"with all your education and authority, to encourage these wretched men when the Government's doing everything it can." Robin had stared at him with his hard blue eyes. "I think you should come and talk to them, Tony. Perhaps if you knew what was happening in Jarrow and South Wales you would see why they needed encouragement." "I'm afraid" he'd answered "that I should not feel justified in indulging my sentimentality at the expense of the unfortunate." Then Priscilla had said abruptly "There's no room for that sort of talk, here, Tony, at this time," and he had left. After that there had been the Spanish War, and with the terrible outrages that he read of each day not only in the Universe, but in non-Catholic papers like the *Mail* he had felt too angry to wish to see them.

Nevertheless, to-day as he made his way downstairs, almost a slim young man in his well-cut tweeds, but for a strange stiffness in the legs, a more kindly memory of the house came over him. The war years had brought about a curious *rapprochement*. A bomb exile from London, he had taken refuge in his wanderings for a

short while at the Mitre and had met his cousins by
chance one morning in the High.   It had taken only
a few minutes for the memory of their disagreements
to be glossed over and then they had found an under-
lying bond in their lack of enthusiasm for the war. Tony
was not, of course, unpatriotic, but he had been a
great Munichite and sometimes when he thought of the
alliances we had been led into he wondered if it was all
quite wise, the Nazis were only half the Devil, as dear
Father Parrott said, and that not the greater half. But
it was more than that, he could not but look back with
excitement to the old days of "the boys on leave," the
hectic fever of "The Bing Boys" and "Romance"—
what was it the girls had sung in that concert party?
"Your arms are our defence, our arms your recompense"
—and now there were hardly any boys on leave, only a
few brave R.A.F. pilots, and he didn't seem to know
any of them.   Priscilla and Robin on their side were
cast in an uncomfortably new role. They had almost
literally "worked their insides out" with hastily snatched
cups of coffee and indigestible sandwiches to release
Ossietsky and imprison Mosley, for United Front, and
"Down the drain with Chamberlain," but now, with
Robin tied to Oxford, there was little to do but combine
with ex-Colonels and Conservative ladies in A.R.P.
and W.V.S., or get hot round the collar listening to
Churchill, for it was still too early in the war to be
building a brave new world. So they really washed up
together quite well for a while, and built a little wall of
family snaps and family jokes to keep the tide of middle
age from the door. Tony had almost succeeded in for-

getting his fears of "Courtwood" in those days, almost, but not quite.

Tony stopped cautiously at the foot of the stairs and peered into the narrow hallway. Too often in the past he had been caught among the mantraps that homely disorder assembled there, barking his shins upon croquet mallets or entangling himself in the spokes of bicycle wheels—how often Uncle Stephen had misquoted "When bicycles stand in the halls," it was one of those little literary flippancies in which the household delighted. Everything seemed so securely smug still that Tony could hardly believe that his cousins were living in the shadow of death and yet it was exactly that which had brought him to "Courtwood" on what might well be his last visit. He had been deeply and genuinely moved by Priscilla's letter, and, at the same time, had felt that faced by the reality of pain and death his relatives might surely at last take off their blinkers and stop trying to fit God's Universe to their own little home-made paper schemes. It provoked and depressed him to find so much unchanged.

Certainly Priscilla's letter had given every ground for belief that the foundations were crumbling. If pain and despair could shed forth rays of hope, then here indeed was the very sun of promise. "You will wonder, Tony, I expect, why I should write to you like this, but it seems so terrible to stand by and see him suffer and to know that I can do nothing"—so she had written and Tony reading the large sprawling handwriting had felt that his chance had come—"The doctors say the operation was a complete failure, and it is only a matter of a

month or so. He is able to go on with his work for the
moment, which is a great help. But there'll be a lot left
over for me to finish, and I feel very proud that he is so
confident of my powers. All the same I feel horribly
afraid of the future loneliness—it is I suppose, the
inevitable price of our great happiness, unfortunately I
am not very good of thinking of life in terms of prices.
I'm sure he would not like it if he knew I was writing
all this to you, but we have agreed that there is no point
in alarming Nick as it would only be, I'm afraid, an
emotional, messy sort of existence, and we're none of us
very good at that"—that they should admit to "not
being good" at so many things, thought Tony, was a
salutary sign—"and so I'm telling you all this, Tony
dear, perhaps because of the old days in the garden here
and of the days on the river." Tony could feel no warm
glow of sentiment at these memories, but he reflected
that there were so many roads by which a poor, weary
soul could find its way to God. "What worries me
most, Tony, is that sometimes I think I've imposed my
will too much upon him—you know how untidy and
muddled he is, not in his thoughts, of course, but in his
ways, and with his books and papers, and I—well you
know what I am. Perhaps he would have liked better
just to have sat about and read and talked—been a kind
of Coleridge. But I expect we all have regrets at these
times, Mother used to worry about laughing at Father's
old spirit rapping. Anyhow I take comfort from the
long row of books sitting in front of me as I write—
books that have influenced events too. A housing expert
was down here last week and he said that Robin's work

was the foundation of all they were doing, and without my system of files and indexes the work wouldn't have been done. . . ." Tony shuddered as he read this passage, he could see the row of books so clearly—hard little, bright covered books full of facts, a dangerous array of so-called scientific knowledge that tried to treat man as a machine. How pitiful that she should still take comfort from the praise of some wretched civil servant! How pitiful that she could still believe in this illusory paradise of refrigerators for all! But still there was quite enough doubt and perplexity and contrition in the letter to give a hope of better things and so, despite Mrs. Fawcett's pleas "that he did more than enough for others" and "that Oxford never did him any good" Tony had appeared once more in the Woodstock Road.

The kindly memories of war-time hospitality were still with Tony as he entered the sitting-room, so that the aridity of taste betrayed in its furnishing did not jar upon him as much as usual. He certainly had no innate liking for oatmeal fabrics and unpolished oaks, he would have preferred *one* long, low glass-fronted bookcase rather than four *walls* of them, whilst Marc's red horses in reproduction did not seem to him adequate pictorial decoration; but still it was an improvement on the smug, satisfied late-Victorian ugliness of Aunt Ethel's day, a bit forbidding and austere, perhaps, but not impenetrably so—or was it that he felt some faint breath here of his own happy chromium-plated 1920's now only permitted to be remembered as "those foolish, far-off days, my dear, when we were, I fear, as vulgar as we were misguided." Whatever the cause he greeted Priscilla with a peculiarly gracious smile when she came in bearing a tray of cocoa and biscuits. How wise he had been to talk only of general matters during last night's depressingly inadequate meal, but now, with care and finesse, he might really succeed in saying something of what was in his mind.

"My dear, a dish of chocolate. I'm obleeged to you," he said, trying hard not to frown at the mauvish grey liquid in his cup, "I quite forgot to tell you that I saw old Ada Lucas the other day in Knightsbridge."

"Did you?" Priscilla answered absently, she found it so difficult to concentrate on anything but Robin at the moment, and Tony's sudden appearance in the house was a particular perplexity for her.

"Yes, my dear, ten times as large as life and four hundred times as ugly. She seems to have eaten through all the alimony which she wrung out of that poor old major and is selling hats in Beauchamp Place. She bought the shop from a friend and, of *course*, there's some terrible law suit about the goodwill and the stock she took over. I longed to tell her that if the hat she was wearing was part of the stock, she had only to appear in court with it to prove *ill* will down to the hilt, but I couldn't get a word in edgeways. She went on and on about her frightful granddaughter—the one who was sick into Mabel Corbett's Sèvres bowl and said she thought it was a chamber—who it seems is ruling the Germans with a rod of iron. Has Nick mentioned meeting her by any chance?"

"He hasn't said anything," replied Priscilla vaguely, "I don't expect he'd be in her set at all."

"You'll send for him to come home, of course," said Tony suddenly and sharply.

"Oh no, Tony, no," cried Priscilla, "Robin and I have talked it over. We've told him, of course, but Robin has asked him especially not to come in view of the importance of his work there, you see he's just in the middle of re-organizing the whole teaching syllabus in the Hochschule."

"Priscilla darling," said Tony and he looked up at her gravely, "you'll forgive me if what I say seems impertinent, but this isn't a *game* that's happening, it's a very important, real thing."

Priscilla seemed like some huge Epstein figure seated with her legs apart, one elbow on her knee, her chin cupped in her hand.

"No, Tony, it's very far from a game," she said, "and its reality's with me every minute of the day, but it isn't *important*, at least Robin and I don't think so. It's all that Robin's done in his life that's important, not this. We've talked it over so often in the past, we're not children you know, so we know where we stand. We've made mistakes, but on the whole we've been on the right lines, beside *that* fact, any feelings of fear or loneliness or doubt, even this beastly physical pain are irrelevant— squalid and unnerving but irrelevant."

"You didn't feel that when you wrote to me, my dear," said Tony quietly.

"Oh, Tony, how can you?" cried his cousin. "Now that *does* shock me. To take advantage of a letter like that, the sort of wretched, hysterical outburst that one hopes so much will never happen, but which always does at these hateful, morbid times."

"So your grief was without reason then," said Tony.

"No, of course not. But that wasn't a letter of grief, it was an outburst of self-pity," answered Priscilla, and then as Tony was about to speak, she hit the arm of her chair and cried, "no, Tony, please. We shall only quarrel."

Tony got up slowly from the oatmeal sofa and stood for a moment, one hand on his corseted hip, the other fingering the rust-coloured window curtain, he gazed at the spotted laurels for some minutes and then turned suddenly towards his cousin.

"Priscilla," he said shrilly, "doesn't it mean anything to you that Robin is a Catholic?"

"A Catholic?" Priscilla asked, "I don't understand. Oh! you mean because those awful parents of his were Catholics for a time."

"No, Priscilla. There's no question of 'for a time,' Robin's parents were *Catholics*, bad Catholics, if you like, but Catholics; and Robin is a Catholic too, he was baptized into the Church."

"But, Tony, Robin didn't know anything about that, and in any case he's never given it a thought from that day to this," and as Tony's long white hands were waved in protest at her *naiveté*, she went on, "Oh, yes, I know what you're going to say. All about baptism and membership of the Church and Catholics having an especial grace, I'm not wholly ignorant. I've heard it all before and we've all said what strength it gave the R.C.s and how logical it was and so on and so on, and very often I've thought of you, because you're about the only Catholic I know well, and sometimes I've even envied you. But now I see what it's all about—Robin's parents passing through one of their crank phrases and Robin happening to be born then and being baptized in the Catholic Church—and you apply all your same arguments by rule of thumb. That's your logic and it's just nonsense." Priscilla's heavy frame was shaking with anger, "It'll be Robin in mortal sin next, I suppose," she said.

"We're not a committee of film magnates, my dear, or whoever the people are who sit about making snap decisions," said Tony. "It's not for you nor me nor the greatest saint in the world to sit in judgment, God alone can do that. I should dispute every belief that Robin cherishes and yours too for that matter, but if you *want* to make impertinent judgments I should say that you've escaped the contamination of your wrong-headed principles quite miraculously. You're certainly far better people than I am. But that isn't the point, even if I thought you were the greatest sinners since Lucifer fell, it wouldn't be either here or there, no one can know the circumstances of a man's life, not even himself, perhaps. It would be easy, for example, to be led into criticism of Robin's parents in this matter, for undoubtedly they did him great wrong, but it would also be very foolish, we must recognize God's infinite wisdom and remember His infinite mercy and leave it at that. Certainly Robin himself has not lived in a world which could help him to see things clearly. After all," and he laughed, " 'Courtwood' is a very dark corner of pagan England. One could only pray and hope. At least so I thought, but your letter made me wonder a little."

"My letter?" echoed Priscilla.

"Yes, my dear, at the risk of annoying you I will repeat—your very human and wonderful letter. In an age in which shoddy thinking is only exceeded by shoddy living one doesn't see many marriages which come near to the meaning of Christian marriage." Tony's voice shook a little, as it did increasingly in old age, when he spoke of motherhood or marriage, "not even, I'm afraid, among those who have been privileged to know better. That's why I've always, despite our many differences, admired you and Robin. Without any guidance you've made a success of marriage that a Catholic couple might envy. You talk about your work and Robin's, but if it was all forgotten to-morrow, as I have no doubt it will be, you've created something far more enduring in the example you have given to Nick. When then, my dear, guided by a sound woman's instinct—a thing no amount of committees can entirely destroy—and by a great love, *you* express doubts about Robin's satisfaction with his life, then I *must* wonder whether perhaps that baptism, which as you say was so long ago, may not be nearer to Robin in his mind than I thought."

As Tony had been talking, Priscilla's bewilderment had grown; it seemed to her as though he was an embodiment of all that people thought of one without one's guessing. He was a nice old thing, and if it had not been so inopportune a time she would have been glad to see him, but he had nothing to do with her life or Robin's, and yet this strange story about them had been going on in his head, even impelling him to leave the comfort of his London flat for the discomfort of their home. She felt exhausted at all the endless projections of herself and Robin that she suddenly saw before her, living out their strange and separate existences in the minds of their friends. Mechanically she said, "I don't understand, Tony. What doubts?" though she could guess wearily at what he would say in answer.

"The doubts, dearest Priscilla, that you so typically described as 'wishing he might have been a Coleridge,' though why you should have to drag Coleridge in, only your staunch North Oxford spirit can explain."

Priscilla got up from her chair and began to replace the cups on the tray.

"I said Coleridge, you know, because I meant Coleridge, that and nothing more. You've done so many acrobatics inside your squirrel's cage, that you've quite forgotten all the antics a monkey can get up to in a bigger one." She spoke as though reproving a precocious child. "The dreams and ambitions of what you call souls, Tony, are so many more than you seem to allow for. When I wrote to you that day, I had been watching Robin's imagination at work building patterns and shapes, some of them rather vague and over-elaborate, but all of them rather interesting. It was one of his talkative days, and I thought of how he might have been a Coleridge instead of a good economist. But it wasn't very sensible of me really, because even if a Coleridge or a Wilde could expand to-day, I doubt if Robin would consider it either the time or the place in history."

"Certainly not for both of them at once." The directness of Priscilla's priggishness was always cloaked in Robin by a touch of whimsicality, but his voice since his illness was less buoyant, more flat. Both Tony and his wife stared at him, and indeed to Tony his cadaverous appearance was a great shock, for he had always secretly admired his cousin's youthful grace. Now, however, the boyish head was like a skull surmounted by a plume of white feathers, and the emaciation of his body was emphasized by his student style of dress. The Adam's apple showed grotesquely above the open neck of his blue linen shirt, even his feet looked pitifully bony in their leather sandals.

"Tony says you're worried about being a Catholic and not having been one," said Priscilla defiantly. Tony moved his hand in protest, but she disregarded him. "*Do you ever think about it Robin? It's nonsense isn't it?*"

In personal matters, Robin was as pacific as his wife was pugnacious, only over social injustice did he ever lose control of his feelings.

"That was kind of you, Tony," he said.

"Kind? What do you mean?" asked Priscilla genuinely, for she was always ready to believe that her husband understood something of which she was ignorant.

"Well, perhaps not kind, but dutiful, and that's really more to the point," Robin replied.

"I know you'll understand my saying, Robin," Tony intervened, "that the whole matter is hardly one to be discussed in this way. Anyhow it was foolish of me to intervene. If you wanted such help there are people far more qualified than I am. People to whom I should be glad to introduce you."

"Thank you," said Robin. "Yes, of course, it's a serious matter, but I should like to ask what gave you the idea?"

"A stupid letter I wrote," said Priscilla.

"Letter? What letter?" said Robin, and then regretted the question. In his present tired and painful condition he did not wish to touch any deep levels that affected his relations with Priscilla, he would prefer to let their marriage fade out on the same relatively successful plane on which it had always existed.

"A silly, hysterical, self-pitying letter. I wrote it in a state after Dr. Mainwaring left."

"It was a very moving letter," said Tony.

"It was good of you to be moved by it," answered Robin icily. It was the greatest anger he felt prepared to allow to his shattered body.

"I wrote it after you had been talking so brilliantly on Friday evening," his wife went on, "and I thought perhaps all my making you orderly and tidy had stopped you from being a great conversationalist like Coleridge and Wilde. It was silly of me, I know."

"I think it was rather sweet," said Robin, "but you need have no fears, I have never envied Coleridge, opium has never attracted me. As for Wilde," he smiled across at Tony, "I've never had any inclination that way either. But I still don't really understand."

"Oh! of course, as soon as Tony saw the letter he thought you might be in doubt about what you'd done in life and then he imagined all this business about the Church."

"Well, darling," said Robin, "it was possibly a more constructive idea than Coleridge and Wilde. I'm afraid though Tony that I remain satisfied not with the amount I have done, God forbid, but with the kind."

"Satisfied with drains and baths and refrigerators?" Tony asked.

"Yes," said Robin, "only with more of them and better ones, and with sickness benefits and secure old age and works committees and," here he smiled again, "the just wage. Strangely enough I did re-read William James the other day, but I'm sorry to say that in all that welter of religious experience I could find nothing to accord with anything I had ever known. I'm sorry, Tony." He returned to Priscilla jovially, "You've forgotten, darling, that that young couple are coming for a drink before lunch."

"Oh dear," Priscilla cried, "all these young people are so awful."

Tony welcomed the diversion as much as his hosts.

"What's this heresy?" he asked, "You to speak ill of the young."

"Well they *are*," said Priscilla, glad to take up a more social tone, "the undergraduates since the war have been absolutely bloody," and she rounded her eyes in childish defiance.

"Priscilla means that their opinions do not accord with ours," said Robin.

The social occasion proved most sticky. It would have taken more than Michael and Harriet Eccleston's rather prim presence to clear the emotional air. There were long silences in which glasses were twiddled and cigarettes refused. Neither Robin nor Priscilla could think of much to ask about Michael Eccleston's experiences in the desert or in Italy, and Tony racked his brain for another possible Wren officer colleague of Harriet's. The failure of his visit had brought all his old feelings of inadequacy back to him, "Courtwood's" triumph was complete. At least, however, on this occasion he could not be said to be out of things, for there was really nothing to be in. Robin and Priscilla were as ill-at-ease as he was, and they seemed determined to confine the conversation to the war—surely, he thought, with a new one in the offing, we could regard the last one as dead. Gradually little undertones in the talk gave him the clue; they were deliberately avoiding general issues, experience had taught them, as Robin had said, that undergraduate opinions did not accord with theirs. Poor Robin and Priscilla, how much they must hate that, and they were too tired to fight the younger generation. Only gradually did the converse dawn on him, however, that at last *he* was on youth's side. When Robin remarked that Michael must find chapel a bore, the young man stroked his moustache and murmured that he doubted if boredom was a possible reaction when something of the kind was so badly needed. Harriet, too, wondered if freedom was quite the issue when one looked at India, after all responsibility was important. They *both* wondered about the death penalty, wasn't abolition rather an easy luxury in the face of social duty? Tony began to purr, he might have been back in Knightsbridge. In desperation Robin got out old snaps, in some of which Harriet's father, a former colleague of his, appeared.

"Oh! look, Michael," cried Harriet, "there's one of

Daddy carrying an incredible banner. He wouldn't dare to show *that* at home."

There were photographs of Robin as a conscientious objector farm labourer in 1916, and pictures of Priscilla and himself relaxing at Fabian Summer Schools in Buxton, and Brighton and Exeter. There was Robin with a Social Democrat mayor being shown the Karl Marx Haus in Vienna—

"One of the few good things the Duke of Windsor did was to insist on seeing that, after Dollfuss came to power," said Robin.

"Rather irresponsible, wasn't it, sir?" asked Michael.

There were United Front groups. "You don't look very united," said Harriet, "you look as though you were about to bite each other."

There were even pictures of the famous rally to feed the Hunger Marchers.

"I should have thought that sort of approach was rather theatrical in dealing with a national problem," remarked Michael.

"They were starving in Wales and in the north," said Priscilla savagely, "they wanted people down here to know about it."

Harriet said, "Oh, of course. No one would blame *them*. Only it seems so terrible that political capital should have been made out of their misery."

"Like the Tories did out of the General Strike," said Robin.

"Well, after all, two wrongs don't make a right. Anyhow I think party politics are rather a dirty game," Michael was quite the gruff ex-officer.

"Yes," Priscilla answered, "so did Hitler."

They managed, however, to end the occasion on an easier note.

As Tony was to lunch at Baliol, he walked with the Eccleston's as far as St. Giles'. He felt completely at ease now; if the house still defeated him on the deeper levels, he had won a complete victory on more surface issues and really, he reflected, to gain the support of young Oxford in his cousins' own home was the capture of an inner citadel. He had not even needed to voice his agreement with the Ecclestons; the atmosphere had been redolent with sympathies. But now he spoke.

"Of course," he said, "you realize that darling Priscilla and Robin were not representative of my generation. A good many of us thought quite differently."

"Oh naturally, sir," said Michael, he loved old world manners.

"I think it's rather pathetic," said Harriet, "and I suppose they *did* do very good work in a way."

"I'm afraid," said Michael, "that so much of it was sentimentalism of a rather dangerous kind. You can't get past Munich, you know."

Even Tony realized there was some confusion here, but still it was on the right lines, so he did not contradict.

"I suppose it's always the same when people live in the past," said Harriet, in a satisfied tone.

"Yes indeed," replied Tony. "Poor Robin and Priscilla are extinct, I'm afraid." He hadn't felt so modern since the first production of "*L'Apres Midi*."

"They're dodos, really, but," he added more kindly, "such darling dodos,"

Necessity's Child

FOUR years ago I still could know the seashore, especially the summer seashore of purple sea anemones, of ribbon weed clear like coal tar soap, of plimsoll rubber slipping upon seaweed slime, of crab bubbles from beneath the rock ledge—but now I have grown up—thirteen years old, too old to make my bucket the Sargasso Sea, too old to play at weddings in the cliff cave, too old to walk with handkerchief falling round my calf from a knee cut afresh each day on the rocks. Now there is only the great, far-stretching sea that frightens me. If I were like other boys, I should be getting to know the sea by swimming in it, treating it as my servant, somewhere to show off my strength, to dart in and out of the waves like a salmon, to lie basking on the surface like a seal. Mummy and Daddy and Uncle Reg can move like that. At one time they tried to teach me to join them, but now they have given me up as hopeless. I can watch their movements and wish to imitate them, but when I am in the water I am afraid, I am so alone there, its great strength is too great, it draws me under. I can lie on the beach and dream—I am Captain Scott watching the sea leopard catch the awkward penguins; I am the White Seal as he swam past the great, browsing sea cows; I am Salar the Salmon as he sported in the weir; I am Tarka the Otter as he learned to swim downstream; above all nowadays I am lying in the sun on the deck of the Pequod with the

Southern Cross above me. But there always comes the moment of fear—Captain Scott has dread in his heart as he reaches the Pole too late; the White Seal grows up to fear the hunter; Salar the Salmon must dart from the jaws of the conger eel; Tarka lies taut beneath the river bank as the hounds breathe overhead; on the Pequod is heard the ominous tapping of Ahab's ivory leg. Even in my dreams I must be afraid, must feel unprotected.

Mummy and Daddy are ashamed of my fears. They play games that are meant to be for my benefit, but they are their games really. I spoilt cricket on the beach as I used to spoil their sand-castles. When we were playing last summer, Mummy called out that she did not want me on her side. "I'm not having Rodney on our side," she said, "I want to win." "We'll have to have you on *our* side, old man," Daddy said, "if your mother doesn't want you. I think we can carry a rabbit, don't you, Reggie?" and Uncle Reggie said, "Yes, you'll have to be the tail, Rodney. With luck it'll be lunchtime before the last man goes in." It was just the same building sand-castles when I was little. Once I started to make a ruined tower. "What on earth is that, darling," Mummy asked me, and when I told her, "Ruined is about right," she said. "Derek, my dear, what can make him suppose that we want a ruined tower when we're building the Clifton suspension bridge?" "Ye olde ruined and medieval suspension bridge, eh Rodney?" said Uncle Reggie. But Daddy just took the sand to build one of his pediments. In the end I used to fetch and carry for them. "Get us some sea-water in that bucket, there's a good little chap," or, "Darling, just dig all round here for me." Sometimes I used to forget about the game and stand dreaming, then it used to be, "Don't stand on the drawbridge, old chap, that'll never do," or, "Darling, if Uncle Reggie takes the trouble to make this marvellous fort for you, I *do* think you might take some interest."

The truth is that I am in the way. I heard Mummy telling Auntie Eileen about it one afternoon in the garden. "Well there it is," she said, "we can never have another and so we must face the situation. But you can say what you like, Eileen, I'm not having a mother's darling around the place. I suppose it's very awful of me to say so, but I realize now that the whole thing was the greatest mistake. Derek and I aren't the sort of people to make parents. We married because we were in love, we still are and we're going to stay that way. We like having fun and we like having it together. Derek doesn't want to come home to someone who's old and tired and scratchy at the end of the day and I intend to see that he doesn't." Auntie Eileen thinks she can make up for it, she's kind to me and when I was little it was nice to play with her. But Mummy's right when she says that she's silly. She doesn't understand anything. She just likes to share silly secrets. "Well, Rodney, what little stories have you been making up to-day?" She likes to show off when people are there, too. She winks at me with her stupid, fat sheep's face. "Rodney and I have lots of little secrets, haven't we?" She made me ashamed when she came down to the Christmas play, talking to Mr. Rogers like that. "I'm not a bit surprised at Rodney's acting so well. You see we've always been rather special friends and we've had our little plays since he was ever so small." But she didn't notice the look on Mr. Rogers' face.

I wish I was back at school. I wish this holiday was over. There'll be nets and missing catches, I know, and the bridge ladder and not knowing the answers in algebra and old Puffin banging his ruler down so that you can't think. "If you can't deal with X and Y, try and think what the answer would be if it was pears and apples, or the beloved pineapple chunks," as if *that* made it any easier. But then there'll be Tony and Gerald to talk to. Gerald said that he would read *Moby Dick* too, when Mr. Rogers told us about it, and even if Tony can't manage it, and lots of it *is* difficult to understand, we can tell him about all the important bits like Ahab's fight with the white whale, and the sea-hawk, and Queequog praying to his idol. We'll all have read *The Wreckers*, too, because Mr. Rogers set it as holiday reading, we'll be able to act lots of it and with any luck they'll let me act Pinkerton. Mr. Rogers said we should read *Barnaby Rudge* for English, it will be the last book I shall read in class at St. Bertram's, because in the autumn I shall be going on to Uppingham. To a public school! Mummy and Daddy like to talk about it, but I try not to listen because I'm so frightened. Oh God don't let me think about it! Oh God don't let me think about it! If I count one hundred and three before I get to the kiosk I shan't ever go to a public school. One, two, three, four, five, six, seven, eight. . . .

"Talking to yourself? That's bad, that's very bad" the thick, unctuous voice sounded stern, but jolly.

Rodney, startled out of his thoughts, stared up at the flabby and rubicund face of Mr. Cartwright, the vicar of St. Barnabas'. "You know what they say about people who talk to themselves, don't you? Just a little bit cracked, getting ready for the looney bin," and Mr. Cartwright laughed with schoolboy glee. "I'm afraid I didn't know I was doing it" mumbled Rodney. "That's no excuse in the eyes of the law" boomed Mr. Cartwright, all mock magisterial severity. "And how have the holidays been? Pretty busy, eh? Gordon and Roger have got a craze," and he dwelt lovingly on what he felt to be the juvenile *mot juste*, "on hockey at the moment. They tell me you don't play. You know I'll let you into a secret if you won't tell the boys," he looked all conspiratorial, "I've no use for the game either. Fast enough, I know, but it always seems to me something of a girl's game. I tell you what though, Mr. Harker's lent the boys the gym at the High School, you must come up one evening for a rag."

Rodney murmured an assent, then, as Mr. Cartwright continued to talk of his sons and the April Fool they had played upon him, he suddenly became panic-stricken at the thought of the commitment. I can't go up there, I won't.

"I'm afraid I shan't be able to come after all" he interrupted Mr. Cartwright breathlessly "you see Mummy's ill and she likes me to be about to help in the house."

"Oh! I'm sorry to hear that," said the vicar, "not seriously I hope. Mrs. Cartwright will want to call and help when she hears."

"Oh please no visitors or telephones at the moment," said Rodney.

"Dear, oh, dear. *You* must keep us posted then. It's a fine thing for you that you can be such a help at this time. A great fellow like you can do a lot to earn your living. You'll be leaving St. Bertram's soon for a wider world, I suppose. Uppingham, isn't it? That's something to look forward to. Though mind you," and his voice took on a confirmation-class note, "it won't be all beer and skittles at first. One gets to be rather a big pot at one's prep school, and unfortunately when one goes on to a public school they don't seem to quite see things that way. But you'll soon settle down. It's just a question," he added with ringing confidence, "of not getting rattled."

He's speaking about it as though it was certain to happen, as though it didn't matter, thought Rodney. How can I make myself not mind going there, if there are people like him about who take all the bullying for granted, who seem to want it. If none of it can happen to me, I won't even let *him* think it can. Aloud he said "I know heaps of other boys there already, so I expect I shall be all right."

"Good show," said Mr. Cartwright, "well, we shall expect to hear great things of you," and with a pat on the boy's shoulder, he set off along the parade.

I've told him two lies, thought Rodney, and they're bound to be found out. It's always happening like that. Why didn't I say that I didn't want his rotten rag in the gym? Why did I have to say I knew people at Uppingham when I didn't? Because you were afraid of his

knowing you were frightened. And now Mummy and
Daddy will find out that I lied and they'll despise me for
it. If I was dying like Thatcher when he had meningitis,
they wouldn't want me always to be with other boys,
they would want to have me with *them*. If Daddy was to
die, I should be very brave and Mummy would be very
proud of me. The schoolroom is filled for evening
prayers when old Puffin calls out loudly "Brent, will
you step outside please, we have some rather serious
news about your father." Whitefaced and tense, but
steady I walk out of the room. Mummy is sitting
weeping in Puffin's study. "I don't need an explanation,
sir, I think I understand. My father is dead!" and then
with my arms round her, "Don't cry, darling, I will try
to be all he would have wanted me to be," and then to
Puffin, "I think, sir, if you could get my mother a little
brandy." Making up horrible daydreams, that's all I
ever do. I can't be any good except in my imagination.
It's not fair, really, there's nothing to be brave about,
when all that is wanted of you is to keep out of the way.
I shall sit in the shelter here and read *The Wreckers* until
long after suppertime and then perhaps they'll wonder
where I am and get worried about me.

The problem of the mysterious cargo of the wrecked
ship was so absorbing that it was some time before
Rodney noticed that he had been joined in the shelter
by two other people. The stout old lady in the heavy
fur coat was the first to speak, "You *must* have an interesting book to be carried away like that," she said. Rodney
decided that with her long face, her tiny eyes and the
warts on her cheek she looked like a huge furry hippo-

potamus. "A really good yarn on a nice spring day. What could be jollier?" said the old gentleman in slow, mournful tones, which seemed somehow accentuated by the downward curve of his long white moustaches and the watery blue of his protruding pug's eyes.

"It's Robert Louis Stevenson's *Wreckers*" said Rodney with some pride.

"Ah!" said the old gentleman "the redoubtable Pinkerton. Somebody you're not familiar with, my dear" he added to his wife, "not unlike that American we met last year who'd patented those revolting and peculiarly useless braces."

"I don't think I should have particularly wanted to read about him," said his wife, "he had such very bad manners. But there I expect it would be different if it was in a book."

"My wife's one of those unfortunate people who can't read," said the old gentleman with great seriousness. The old lady protested laughingly and an expression of puzzled concern appeared on Rodney's face. "Well it's almost true" the old gentleman went on, "she never learnt the delight of books until she was too old. Now when I was your age I lived half my time in the stories I read, as I've no doubt you do. I remember being D'Artagnan for weeks on end—a great, swaggering Gascon fellow, I'm not sure it wasn't then that I grew these moustaches. One thing I am sure of, though, I didn't keep to the book exactly. I remember I always saved milady from the block at the last minute. I know, of course, that she wasn't exactly a nice person, but still it's always the mark of a cad to refuse to help a beautiful woman when she's in trouble."

"I love the chapters where milady seduces Felton," said Rodney.

"Ah! yes a nice juicy bit," said the old gentleman, looking sideways at his wife's shocked expression, "there's no need for alarm, my dear, the word seduce is used only in a very general sense, to imply dereliction of duty and that sort of thing, you know. But my wife does like *one* book" he turned to Rodney "our grandchildren read it to her last winter, and that's *Wind in the Willows*. Of course, she fell in love with Toad."

"I didn't," protested the old lady "I thought he was odious." "Oh! he wasn't really," said Rodney, "He was really a nice, kind sort of person, only he boasted rather a lot."

"Yes, yes," said the old gentleman, "We're none of us free from weaknesses, not even you, my dear. And then he was a pioneer of motoring, though whether that's on the credit side I'm not so sure. However he had a proper sense of his superiority to the teaching profession, which our friend here no doubt shares. 'The clever men at Oxford know all there is to knowed'," he recited, laughing heartily.

" ' But there's none of them knows half as much as intelligent Mr. Toad' " finished Rodney and he began to laugh too.

His enjoyment was suddenly halted, however, by the lady's next remark.

"I expect you read lots of books aloud to *your* mother," she said.

Rodney paused some moments before answering.

"Yes" he said at last "you see Mummy's an invalid and she depends a lot on me."

"I'm sure you're a great help to her," said the old lady "what does your father do?"

"Daddy's a solicitor" replied Rodney. "Poor Daddy" he added with a deep sigh.

"That's a very large sigh for so small a person," said the old lady.

"I was just thinking how difficult it is when people don't understand each other. Daddy's such a kind man really, only he gets so angry because Mummy's always snapping. It's only because she has dreadful pain to bear, but Daddy doesn't seem to understand. That's what makes him drink so. When he gets drunk he says dreadful things to Mummy and then she wishes she could die."

"Never mind, my dear," said the old lady "if I understand how your Mummy feels, having you about will make life worth living."

"That's what Daddy says" Rodney went on in increasingly excited tones "We had wonderful walks together in the country and along the seashore. He knows all about birds and fishes and makes everything so interesting. If only Mummy knew what he was like then, oh! I wish I could make them understand each other. I think I'm the only person who could."

The old gentleman left off drawing lines in the gravel with his walking stick. He looked quizzically for a moment at Rodney, then he said drily, "Making human beings understand one another can be quite a difficult task."

Rodney's look of bewilderment as he replied was appealing in its innocence. "Oh! I know how difficult it will be, and after all I am only a child."

The old gentleman's tone was more kindly, as rising from the seat he patted Rodney's shoulder, "I shouldn't worry too much if I were you, grown-up people are very strange creatures" he said "they often seem to be in a bad way, but it's amazing how quickly they pull out of it. Well, we must be going, my dear," he added.

The old lady bent down and kissed Rodney's forehead, then she produced a visiting card from her handbag. "If you're ever in need of a friend, this is my name and address" she said, "I shall always think of you as a very brave boy."

It was well after teatime when Rodney returned home, but Mrs. Brent did not appear to notice that he was late. For a moment as he saw her he remembered his lies to the vicar and wondered with dread whether Mrs. Cartwright had rung up. But his trained eye soon saw from his mother's face that no storm was brewing, and with long acquired habit he pushed his fears aside. It hasn't led to trouble yet, he thought, perhaps if I cross my fingers it never will. "Please God, if it's all right this time I'll never tell any more stories," he murmured.

Mummy was wearing her black costume with the diamond shoulder clip, he noticed, and the black hat with the cockfeathers that curled over the ear. That meant that Daddy and she must be going out. They had only been in to dinner four times during the holidays and then there had been visitors so that he had to have supper on his own. If only they would talk to him occasionally. Of course, Mummy *did* sometimes, but only if there was nobody there, and *usually* if they were alone, she would say "Thank goodness! an afternoon to ourselves. Now I can get on with something. I hope you've got things to do, Rodney, because I really must get this finished before Daddy comes home and I don't want to be constantly interrupted." Anyhow Auntie Eileen was here for her to talk to this evening. Certainly no one could want a better listener, he thought, as he watched his aunt's pale moonface with its look of constant surprise, the eyebrows raised and the mouth eternally rounded and ready with exclamations of "Oh!" or "No!" to greet the speaker, her large ear-rings jangling with interest.

"Quite honestly, Eileen, I think she must have been canned" his mother was saying, "She's never a good player, but to go up five in a major suit, when she didn't even hold the top two honours, *and* they were vulnerable. Of course Derek was *furious*. I've promised him we'll never go there again. But it's a frightful bore, because she's been so useful over petrol coupons."

"Oh! Vera, how maddening for you!" said her sister-in-law.

"Yes it is rather, isn't it? Actually, of course, Derek's bridge is so much too good for this town, that it's rather a bore playing anyway. You should see the look on the poor lamb's face sometimes when one of these old girls makes some terrible call. Anyhow the summer's coming now so that with tennis and cricket there won't be much time for bridge.   You know the new road-house has opened on the London Road?"

"No!" said Eileen "Really? I didn't know."

It was amazing how few things his aunt *did* know Rodney reflected.

"Yes, my dear, and it's really awfully gay.   We're motoring out there this evening after drinks at the Graham's.   Derek's crazy to take up dancing in a big way again.   He adores all this old-time dancing.   So the summer programme will be pretty full.   There really *does* look to be a chance of our getting abroad at the end of August.   Derek says all the money restrictions mean nothing if you know the ropes."

"Rodney will like that" said Aunt Eileen.

"My dear," replied Mrs. Brent "I honestly think it would be madness to take him.   Nothing could be less amusing for a child than a Paris holiday, and it wouldn't be terribly fair on us.   No, thank goodness!   The house-master at Uppingham has been amazingly kind about it, he's quite willing for him to arrive there a few weeks early and be a sort of paying guest.   There'll be other boys there, too, which will be very good for him."

"Oh Mummy please!" Rodney cried "Don't make me go there in the holidays.   It'll be awful, I know it will."

"My dear child, there's no need to get excited.   We're not proposing to send you to prison or something.   It'll be a marvellous chance to get to know some of the boys before term begins.   You'll be one up on the other new boys."

"Rodney can come to me, Vera, if he likes," and

Auntie Eileen wrinkled her nose intimately at her nephew, "We'd have grand times."

"There you are, Rodney. You can go to Auntie Eileen's, though I'm not sure it wouldn't be better if you were to be with other boys."

"I don't *want* to go to Auntie Eileen's," Rodney almost shouted. "I want to be with you and Daddy."

"Well, I'm afraid you'll have to want. Daddy and I are going abroad. And now apologize to your aunt for being so rude." It was no good putting everybody against you thought Rodney, so he said "I'm sorry, Auntie Eileen." Then suddenly he kicked at the table "But everything's so jolly dull, I get so bored and that makes me cross."

"What have you been doing this afternoon that bored your lordship so?" said his mother.

"Talking to an old lady and gentleman on the front."

"Well really! Rodney. With hundreds of other children in the town you spend the afternoon talking to some old couple and then you say you're bored. I give up!"

"What about your book?" said Auntie Eileen "You're not the person to be dull if there's a book about."

"Oh it's all right" said Rodney "but I'm tired of reading."

"Why not make up a story for yourself" said Auntie Eileen. "That ought to be great fun and then you can tell it to me."

"Don't spoil the child" said his mother and she began to tell her sister-in-law of their holiday plans.

Half an hour later Rodney's father returned. "Hullo

Eileen," he said to his sister, "What's the best news?"
He leant over his wife's chair and kissed her, running
his hands down her breasts. "Had a good day, Tup-
pence?" he said. His wife's somewhat hard, carefully
made-up face softened as she answered "This is the best
moment." "Same here" he replied, smiling boyishly.
"How's the world treating you, old son?" he called to
Rodney. "He's been an absolute horror" said Mrs.
Brent. "Bad show" said her husband. "We must be
moving, darling." "You look tired, sweet" said Mrs.
Brent. "I am a bit" said her husband, "Then I shall
drive," "I won't say no" and he gave her a smack on
the bottom as he pushed her out of the room "Pass along
the car there" he called.

"Will you be all right, Rodney, while I get your
supper?" said Auntie Eileen "Then we can have a nice
long chat." "I'm busy making up a story like you told
me" said her nephew and he smiled to himself.

A quarter of an hour later when Auntie Eileen returned bringing a cup of Bovril and some jam tart on
a tray, Rodney was sitting in the chair, his body tense
and his face white and strained

"Rodney, darling, what is the matter?" she cried
"Oh! it's so horrible" the boy said, his eyes rounded, "I
couldn't tell Mummy. I can't tell anyone ever."

"You can tell *me*, darling."

"Oh I do so want to. But if I do, you'll tell Mummy.
Promise if I tell that you'll keep it a secret."

"Of course, of course I promise," said Auntie Eileen
with relish.

"It happened this afternoon with that old gentleman"

said Rodney speaking in an excited, staccato voice "he looked so nice, Auntie, and then he showed me pictures, horrible, beastly pictures."

"Oh! my darling" said Auntie Eileen "how dreadful! what a wicked, wicked man," then she added "But I thought you said there was an old lady with him, had she gone away or what?"

There was a short silence and then

"No, Auntie" said Rodney bitterly "No she was there. She just laughed and said they had lots more like that at home and I'd better come back and see them, but I ran away. Promise, promise you'll never tell anyone, it was all so dreadful I don't want to think about it ever again."

"I wish I knew what was right" said Auntie Eileen, but at Rodney's look of alarm, she added "Very well, darling, it'll be our secret, a secret we'll just forget. But I shall always think of you as a very brave boy."

The sea swings away from me now, brown and sandy in patches, but without light, grey and cold. It heaves and tosses and lashes itself into white fury, as it crashes and thunders against the breakwater. It flies into a mist that sprays against my cheeks. But always, however the waves may rush forward, tumbling over each other to smash upon the beach, the sea swings towards me and away from me. I am sitting upon a raft and the calm, level water is swinging me so, back and forward. It is the Pacific Ocean everywhere, clear and green. Over the side of the raft I can see deep, deep down to strange,

coloured fishes and seahorses and coral. I am all alone
"alone on a wide, wide sea." Mummy and Daddy have
gone down with the ship, spinning round and round
like the "Pequod", See! She sinks in a whirlpool and I
am shot out, far out, alone on this raft. The heat will
scorch and burn me, "the bloody sun at noon," and
thirst and the following sharks. Don't let me be alone
so, don't let me think of that. But now the sea is moving,
violently, wildly in high Atlantic waves. I am lashed
to a raft, the sea is swinging me roughly, up on the
crest so that the wing of the albatross or the seahawk
brushes my cheek, raucous screams are in my ears,
hooked beaks snap at my eyes, and now down, down
into the trough where the white whale waits. Mummy
and Daddy have gone down with the ship. It crashed
and broke against the glass-green wall, the name Titanic
staring forth in red letters as it reared into the air.
Mummy's black evening dress floated on the surface
of the water and her shoulder showed white as she was
sucked down. But I am left alone, tied to the raft,
numbed, frozen, choking with the cold, or again, as it
sails relentlessly on towards the next floating green
giant, dashing me to pieces against the ice as I fight
with the ropes too securely tied.

Christmas Day in the Workhouse

THEA was showing one of the new girls how to mark the personnel cards when Major Prosser came in. She continued the demonstration without turning round, not because she thought the work of more importance than the Head of Section's visit, but because she guessed that his sense of his own position would be more flattered by assuming it so. After four years at the Bureau, actions tended to be guided by such purely personal considerations. Where all other values had been effaced by isolation and boredom, only sexual conquest or personal advantage remained as possible goals; most of the time Thea found only personal advantage within her range, but at a certain cost in hysteria she had made quite a success of it—she was, after all, the only woman head of a subsection under the age of thirty.

"Directed staff are marked green for sick leave, volunteers blue, established officers red," she explained, and as she looked at the new girl's pallid skin, she wondered if green had been purposely chosen for the conscripts. She tried very hard to treat these bewildered and unattractive girls with kindness. Sometimes, however, a bitter despair would break through the deadness with which she had insulated herself from the place, and in her anger at the naive enthusiasm with which *she* had first volunteered for the work, she would turn against those who had only come under duress. At such times she would dwell with satisfaction upon these sickly suburban ewe lambs—green-faced girls with pebble glasses, protruding teeth and scurfy shoulders who had been hunted from the protecting parental arms to be sacrificed upon the pyre of communal existence. In fact, of course, as she fully realized, this monotony of ugliness was simply the ready response of the Ministry of Labour to the Bureau's call for "clever girls."

"For the dying, the dead, and those yet unborn, we use black," she went on. It was a joke she had inherited from her predecessor who had thought it out way back in 1939, but as she made it she realized that it was not quite Tim Prosser's sort of remark. It reflected, if only faintly, a certain cynicism towards the Bureau which he preferred only to reserve for expansive moods with his immediate subordinates. All the "old faithfuls" among the girls laughed obediently, and Joan Fowler even managed to impart a special note of devotion towards Thea into her little giggle.

Major Prosser's laugh was really more of an impatient cough. He was beginning to see this devotion to work as lèse-majesté rather than a compliment.

"Have you got Braddock's card there?" he said abruptly. He always used the girls' surnames when he wished to wound the remnants of humane feelings to which Thea clung as the last plank of her self-respect.

"Daphne's card?" she replied on a lingering note, as she tried to puzzle out what he was after.

"Yes, yes," Major Prosser was impatient. "The girl

with the migraines and the excess charm." He liked
Thea's competence, but he genuinely despised her
gentility and what he called her "blasted hard-boiled
virginity."

Anxious to oblige, the new girl handed the card to
him directly. He gave her a friendly, boyish smile that
reminded her of her Daddy.

"Away since September," he said sharply, "I say,
Thea, you ought to have asked me for a replacement
ages ago. Establishment's no sinecure at the best of
times, but carrying passengers!" and he looked all
admiration for her silent self-sacrifice. "Let's see, who
can we give you? I know—Turnbull. I'll see Room 6
straight away."

My God! thought Thea, so that's it. As soon as he
laid a new wench—increasingly she found herself using
the "tough" language affected by her superiors—there
was always a shift round of staff. He'd put his new little
bit in charge of room 6 and now he'd got to weed out
the duds for her. He would have his work cut out in finding a home for Turnbull, whose black frizz with its
bleached streak made her absence from evening shift to
have a bit of fun with the messengers seem somehow
more noticeable than in "quieter" girls.

"Thank you, Tim," said Thea sweetly. The constant
use of Christian names among the heads and sub-heads
was one of the many external signs of the splendid,
amateur, wartime spirit with which they were making
rings round the inflexible efficiency of the enemy, *and*
having fun in doing it. Though Thea had no doubts of
the truth of this claim to improvised genius, she often

found its conscious expression embarrassing. She was,
however, rapidly learning the language by which modesty,
reserve and reticence can be widely advertised.

"Thank you, Tim, I don't think there'll be any need,"
she went on, "Joan Fowler had a letter from Daphne
saying she would be back within a fortnight. That's
right, isn't it, Joan?"

Joan was so delighted that Thea should have turned
to her for support that she blushed wildly and her
genteelly distorted vowels tumbled over one another in
an effort to please.

"Oh, yes, Thea, she's ever so much better, really
almost all right, and her doctor says that as long . . ."

Major Prosser laughed to disguise his disgust at Joan's
lack of sex-appeal. "That's not perhaps quite the
official report," he said, "in any case," and he looked
round the room somewhat venomously, "a drop of new
blood might be a very good idea. We all get a bit stale,
anaemic. . . ."

But Thea was ready for such a favourite generalization,
and quoted another of his loved phrases back at him.

"Except, Tim, that in Establishments we have a highly
integrated group of specially picked personnel." She
knew the phrase from his last report to the chief. He
took the joke against himself with a "good sport" smile,
but she could see he was getting angry.

"Well, we'll talk about it later," he said.

Thea decided that the moment had come to push her
victory home, "I don't suppose it matters," she said,
"but in the report I did for the Duce"—it was their jolly
name for the chief, originally bestowed in bitter con-

tempt, but wisely accepted by him as a piece of family
fun—"saying why the section needed more staff I did
mention that we never cared to move people from one
job to another."

Major Prosser was already somewhat alarmed by the
difficulties of justifying his request for forty new personnel
— a request made because other sections were increasing
—so that the blow was a telling one. Nevertheless, Thea
reflected, she would probably have to put up with
Turnbull's bleached streak, for unless she was prepared
to make a row about it, Tim could always override her
wishes.

"No Christmas decorations yet?" he asked, dismissing
the matter.

"We're putting them up to-morrow morning," said
Thea. "We've got some wonderful caricatures this
year."

"One of me, I hope," said Tim.

"Well, yes," laughed Thea, "show him what you've
done, Stephanie."

If Tim had been expecting giggles and shy refusal, he
was sadly disappointed. Stephanie ignored him altogether, but taking the drawing from a folder on her
table, she handed it to Thea.

"I've got to colour the uniform still," she remarked
in her offhand, dead voice. Tim looked at her long
slender figure and her neatly rolled straight gold hair in
fury and misery. He was always telling his cronies that
these cold bitches with *Tatler* backgrounds weren't
worth laying, "their bed manners are so bloody awful,"
he used to say amid roars of laughter at the local, but

lust and snobbery were too powerful to be resisted in her presence. Even his vanity could not fail to see the bank manager disguised in a uniform which her caricature of him underlined.

"Very good," he said laughing, "I wonder about the moustache though, it's a shade too neat for mine."

Stephanie looked at him for a second "No," she said considering, "I don't think so. I took it from one of those hair cream advertisements."

After Tim had gone, Joan Fowler came and fussed round Thea. "Oh, poor you," she said, "it's absolutely monstrous making you take that awful Turnbull on. I hate all these new people. I'm sure we got much more work done when there were only a few of us. Do you remember, Thea, when there was only you and me and Penelope, and then Stephanie came and poor Daphne. Of course, I think it's been *much* worse since Prosser came. A girl in Room 6 told me last night it was simply *frightful* since he'd pushed that creature of his in there. You don't think he'd ever try to do that here, do you? Oh, but he, *couldn't*, not when you've made so much of Establishments. But then you simply can't tell *what* he might do. If he *did* try to push anyone new in here, I bet you anything nobody would work for them. Even these new girls are frightfully keen on working for you."

If Joan seized any occasion to surround Thea with a fog of vague perils and implied intrigues, it was not from hostility but from an ill-defined feeling that it united them more closely, made her own protective devotion more necessary—locked in each other's arms for safety they could float for ever upon a buoyant sea of treacly emotion. Unfortunately, however tonic such emotions might be to Joan, Thea only felt their stickiness sucking her down. Luckily, her experience as guide leader in her father's parish had taught her to keep such silliness in check.

"Don't forget you're chart-checker to-day, Joan," she said. "We keep a half-day chart for every section," she explained to the new girl. "Green and red for the two shifts, purple for those on half-days. That's if it's working properly. At the moment Joan's got more than half the section marked on leave." A little snub worked wonders with these stupid girls, though, really, she had to admit that Joan's devotion was less revolting than the so-called normal attitude that Tim Prosser and the others professed so loudly, a normality that apparently classed human beings with pigs. The nostrils of her bony Roman nose dilated and her thin faintly coloured lips compressed as she thought of it. For a few seconds she imagined the moment of release from it all, and how Colin would be both disgusted and amused, and then the horrible realization of Colin's death surged through her head. It was one of those appalling failures of memory that occurred, thank God, increasingly less since his 'plane had crashed two years before.

Despite the freezing wind that blew across the dismal meadows, where each month saw less trees and more concrete buildings, the atmosphere in the canteen with its radiators and fluorescent lighting was stifling. The white coats of the waitresses were splashed with scraps of food and gravy stains; around their thickly lipsticked mouths, their cheeks and chins shone greasy and sweaty. The young technician who sat opposite to Thea spat fragments of potato as he talked to his girl friend. She pushed aside her plate and decided to leave before the roof of her mouth was completely caked in suet. What a prelude to a Mozart concert! she thought. Nothing in her education had ever allowed her to bridge the gap between the material and the cultural.

And yet in some curious way they did get entwined that night. The concert hall was packed when she entered and for a few moments she thought with depression that she would have to stand; of course, with the Jupiter to listen to, she was not likely to mind, but she felt very exhausted. Then suddenly she saw Stephanie's delicate hand beckoning to a seat beside her. How cool and restful her large grey eyes and sleek golden hair seemed above the plain cable-stitch jumper and rope of pearls. Thea felt glad, when she looked round the room at the vulgar evening frocks, that she too had not "changed." She was not quite sure that her angora jumper was exactly right, but at any rate her pearls—a twenty-first birthday present from Daddy—were really good. Throughout the Overture to Figaro and the Jupiter she had no mind for anything but the music; for she had heard it often enough to be thinking all the time how important it was to know what was coming, otherwise one never really saw the relation of all the parts to each other. The piano concerto that followed was more difficult, and though she tried hard to listen for the themes she found her thoughts wandering.

It was amazing, she reflected, how one person of the right sort could help to make life tolerable. All the vulgarity, the intrigue, the anxiety that surrounded her life at the Bureau seemed to vanish in Stephanie's presence; but that, of course, was because she was so detached, so completely above them. Breeding did make a difference, there was no doubt of it. Not, Thea thought, that she had a reverence for titles in the vulgar, snobbish way that made so many of the girls excited when they saw Stephanie's picture in the *Tatler*. Half of the people in the *Tatler* were appalling, spending their time at night-clubs and theatres, when the country needed them; but the real aristocracy were quite different, living quietly in the country and doing so much good. The proof of it was, of course, that she'd never had one moment's trouble with Stephanie from the day she joined the section. She knew she had a job to do and she did it, which was exactly what one would have expected of course, and she did it so coolly and efficiently too, although she was only twenty, and had beauty that would have turned any other girl's head. With the sound of the piano as an accompaniment, little pictures began to pass before Thea's eyes. She knew Stephanie's home, Garsett House, well from the outside; she used to pass the lodge gates in the bus from Aunt Evelyn's into Taunton, and she had seen the Countess once at a meet of the stag-hounds near Minehead. Now she saw herself on a horse like Ropey only better, laughing and talking with Stephanie who looked almost haughty in her habit and with her riding whip; or coming down a broad staircase in a plain black evening dress with her pearls, her arm round Stephanie's waist. Stephanie, of course, was in a simple but lovely white frock. Black and white, she pulled herself together as she thought of the advertisement. The slow movement was lovely, but perhaps a little long. It was difficult to imagine the inside of Garsett just from the lodge gates; and Thea felt more safe as she saw Stephanie at the Rectory, galloping on Ropey, for, of course, she would not mind his being old and short-winded; or, even better, laughing at the strange old hats and frocks in the dressing-up box in the nursery. How pleased Mummy would be with her new friend!

When they came out after the concert Thea almost gasped at the beauty of the moonlight on the snow-covered lawn. After a week's hard frost, the wind was warmer, and already everywhere around them the snow was falling from the branches of the trees with strange, sudden, little popping noises, that relieved the frozen tension. And then, "How beautiful it is," Stephanie said, so that Thea almost jumped at the strange unity of their thoughts. They sat waiting in their bus—for their billets were in the same direction—while a crowd of noisy girls from the dance hall climbed into the back seats. Thea, turning round with horror at the sacrilege, saw Turnbull in a dreadful gold lamé evening dress, her bleached streak fallen across her eyes. "When I say I love you," she was crooning, "I want you to know, it isn't because of moonlight, although moonlight becomes you so." Thea had almost decided to demand silence, when suddenly she saw Stephanie's hair gleam pale golden-green in a haze of moonbeams. Of course, these jazz tunes were very frightful, but in a sense they were the folk music of the age, and she could not help dwelling on the phrase "moonlight becomes you so," it was strangely like something in a ballad.

"I don't think I can bear to-morrow's party," said Stephanie suddenly, "Penelope Rogers has bought a special box of Christmas jokes." She looked at Thea quizzically, and they both burst out laughing almost hysterically. Stephanie was the first to recover. "You're tired, Thea," she said, "After the way that wretched little man bothered you to-day. Do you have to come in to-morrow?" and she laid her long fingers on Thea's arm.

"Oh! I think I must" said Thea "but I'm having a quiet Christmas dinner at the billet in the evening."

"You're lucky," laughed Stephanie, "my people have gone away. I shall cook myself an omelette and go to bed."

"You'll like that, I expect."

"Oh, I don't know. I'm rather fond of a Christmas celebration as long as it's not at the Bureau."

"You wouldn't care to come to us, would you?" asked Thea boldly. "It'll be very quiet, only me and my billetor. She's a dear," she was about to add that Mrs. Owens was a doctor's widow when she wondered if that was exactly the kind of thing that would be of interest to Stephanie, so she said rather pointlessly, "she's a widow. Do come."

"Thank you," said Stephanie, "I think I should like to," and then, almost abstractedly, she added, "You do know, don't you, Thea, what a compensation working for you has been? Compensation for the Bureau being so bloody, I mean."

It seemed to Thea as though she floated through the gates of the billet—with their brass plate, last remnant of the late Dr. Owens—and on up the drive, a cold, white river of moonshine. At any ordinary time she would have recoiled from the melting snow as it seeped through her stockings, for her fastidious feelings revolted from any unfamiliar physical touch, but to-night she was dancing on a lake of glass. No happiness, however, could allow her to forget the consideration due to others, so she removed her shoes most carefully as she closed the front door.

"Thea!" Mrs. Owens called from her bedroom upstairs, "is that you?"

It was a nightly repeated ritual that usually formed the final torture of Thea's tiring and nerve-racked days, but to-night. "Yes, Mrs. Owens. Can I come in for a moment?"

She lay back in the armchair by the old lady's bed and ran her hand sensuously over the soft pink eiderdown, just as she did in the rare, happy, midnight "confabs' with Mummy, when Daddy was visit-preaching.

"Does anybody in the world make such perfect Ovaltine?" she cried, as she helped herself from the little spirit stove by the bedside. "Oh, isn't it nice that Christmas is here?" she asked.

"I wish I could do more to make it brighter for you" said Mrs. Owens. "I think it's a shame they don't send you all home. I've made the sausage rolls for you to take to-morrow. I'm afraid they won't go very far. I nearly let the pastry burn. I've been so excited all day. I've had a letter from Stephen, and he's getting leave in the New Year."

"Oh! darling!" cried Thea, "I'm so pleased," and she leaned over and kissed the old lady.

Mrs. Owens was quite surprised by the warmth of her embrace. "We'll have a real celebration to-morrow evening," Thea said, "you must open a bottle of that champagne. Oh, and I've asked someone to come to dinner—Stephanie Reppington."

"That beautiful girl whose picture was in the *Tatler*? Oh, dear I'm afraid we shan't be grand enough." It was one of Mrs. Owens' constant fears that she would not be able to live up to the social standards of her "war-time child."

"Oh Stephanie's not like that," Thea protested, "she's tremendously simple and genuine. I know you'll like her."

"My dear," said Mrs. Owens, "you know that any friend of yours is welcome here," and she smiled so sweetly. It was the most wonderful Christmas Eve, just like a fairy story.

By Christmas afternoon the Establishment Room had been quite transformed, and everything was ready for the tea party. Each plywood table was covered with a lace-edged cloth, and right across the centre of the big middle table, where the adding machines usually stood, ran a row of little pots of holly made so cleverly from tinfoil and decorated with little cut-out black cats in bedsocks. A whole collection of "In" and "Out" trays had been lined with paper doyleys and filled with every sort of delicious cake and sandwich—Thea's sausage rolls and Penelope's dainty bridge rolls filled with sandwich spread, Helen's raspberry fingers and little pyramids of chocolate powder and post toasties that Joan Fowler called "Coconut Kisses": the extra sugar ration of months had gone into the display. Caricatures of everybody were pinned on the walls, and some drawings of cuties modelled on "Jane" from the *Daily Mirror*, but less sexy and more whimsical. It had proved very difficult to fit the branches of holly and evergreen to the blue tubular lighting, but by a united effort it had been done; whilst from the central hanging light there swung an enormous and rather menacing bunch of mistletoe. Stephanie had brought six bottles of peaches in brandy from Fortnum's and they stood in uncompromisingly lavish display on the table by the window, until at the last minute Joan Fowler decided to decorate them with crackers and some silver "stardust" that flew all over the room and stuck to everyone's clothes. At four sharp visitors from other rooms and sections began to arrive.

Never was the dissimilarity, the lack of basic compatibility of the staff of the Bureau more apparent than on such customarily festive occasions as Christmas. Compelled by convention to put aside "shop" talk and the gossip of personalities which surrounded their working hours, the tightly welded machine parts soon collapsed into a motley collection of totally disparate individuals. The service officers found it impossible to continue to suggest that they were really intellectuals; the business-men's service talk creaked badly; whilst the assumptions of business toughness among the dons and school-masters was patently laughable. The women of all ages and classes, who so outnumbered the men at the Bureau, glimpsed with shame something of their failure to preserve the standards of glamour and charm normally offered to the other sex; they saw for a moment that in their fatigue and absorption with routine they had forgotten to turn the males out of the dressing room before it was too late. Everywhere in the room the regulation masks of brightness and competence were slipping, and from behind them peeped forth pre-war faces, pale after so much confinement, and blinking a little at the strange light in which they were seeing the accustomed surroundings, but individual, shy, and faintly disgusted with their colleagues. Heaven knows to what anarchy the discipline of years might have slipped, for an hour or more must pass before the circulation of free beer would allow the tough, brassy, devil-take-the-hindmost gang to assume their wonted leadership, but luckily there was another stable, welding element for whom tea and buns was a familiar signal to take control. From Low Church and Chapel, from C.I.C.U. and O.I.C.U., from the hockey field and the football ground—"God who created me nimble and light of limb"—they were there when needed. All difference, all shyness, was dissolved in the rich strains of "Holy Night" from manly baritones that were all but tenors, from contraltos in pious hootings, from the sweet sopranos of girls with nice home backgrounds.

Unity was for a moment endangered when the girl who ran the Music Club got together with the polo-sweatered organist and tried to raise the artistic tone—it was, after all, the cultural end of England's war service. They just managed to steer through "All under the Leaves," but broke down badly on "Lullay my liking," when once more the fine old strains with the good old words floated forth, and soon they had sunk from Oxford Book of Carols to plain A. and M.

Tim Prosser, like many of the heads, felt rather out of it. But he smiled patronizingly as he always did when things took a religious turn; and even sang feebly once or twice, when old favourites like "Once in Royal David's city" made their appearance. After a decent interval he turned to his favourite occupation of teasing flirtation. As a result of working with "highbrows" he had grafted a certain "clever" undergraduate diction on to his old bank technique with curious results.

"I'm surprised, Pamela," he said, to his girl friend— it was part of the ritual always to repeat their Christian names, "that a fine upstanding example of female emancipation like yourself should wear those outward and visible signs of servitude," and he gave her earrings a little tug that made her wince.

"Oh, stop it," she cried, "you're hurting."

"Stop it," he copied her in falsetto, "does the slave bid her master to cease his attentions? Does Fatima cry to Bluebeard, 'hold, enough.' Pamela!" and he looked stern—"I'm afraid that your visit to London has done you no good."

"You're the end," said Pamela.

"The end, Pamela, the end. You really must enlarge your vocabulary. Now the middle, Pamela, or the beginning, why not try them for a change?"

"Oh stop talking nonsense" protested the girl. "I know, Pamela, I know. 'Ow I do go on, as the tart said to the sailor. But it's nothing to how I *shall* go on, Pamela, if you wrinkle your nose up at me like that. Not that it is different by an inch from any other nose, a hair's-breadth shorter perhaps than Cleopatra's, but then you see, Pamela, like Mark Antony, I'm funny that way," and with this he pinched her thigh.

Thea, who was standing nearby, tried not to give them the satisfaction of seeing her look the other way. Not that vulgarity could upset her this afternoon. Stephanie had brought her peach offering directly to her and they had stood for a moment side by side. When the singing started, the girl had smiled, "It's easier really not to believe it's happening" she had said, and Thea, laughing, had agreed. A few minutes later Stephanie had slipped away, and Thea stood by a window, gazing out on to the wet shiny asphalt paths as though her dreams were reflected in their mirrored surface. She smiled gently at some of her girls from time to time, and, after Stephanie had left, even joined in one of the carols. It was not the sort of singing that would have been favoured at the Rectory—all too hearty and muscular for her father's almost Tractarian taste—so that, happy as she was she could not feel quite "at home"; she was, therefore, dissociated enough to notice the strained, red face of one of the new conscripts. Clearly the simple emotion of the carols had brought "home" all too near. Thea's kindly impulses were liberated by her happiness, and, additionally urged by a personal horror of any public scene, she crossed the room, took the girl by the arm and led her out before the pent-up sobbing had attracted much attention.

The empty workrooms, with their litter of papers and tin lids full of cigarette stumps, were not ideal rest rooms, but at last Thea found one with a battered cane armchair. Here she deposited the hysterical girl, provided her with a cigarette and a copy of *Picture Post*, and left her comparatively restored. A faint ray from the dying winter sun shining upon the wet leaves of the laurels tempted Thea to take a turn through the shrubbery.

She had never been a light-hearted girl, had always walked a tightrope across chasms of social anxiety and private phobia, and, since Colin's death, she had been ceaselessly battling to keep within her strict limits of propriety the violent anger and frustration into which it had plunged her. Now, therefore, that this sudden release from isolation had come, she was constrained by habit to savour it in quietude rather than to laugh and sing out loud as her excited senses urged. She sat on the garden seat under the high cypress hedge that cut the shrubbery in two, and gave herself up to hazy pictures of the future, as she had not dared to do for over two years. She had just been dissuaded by Stephanie's good sense from foolish investment of the proceeds of the little hat shop they had both been so successfully running for some years in Brook Street, when she heard voices approaching from the other side of the cypress hedge. It was the sound of her own name—how often had her self-consciousness imagined this over the last years, but this time she was not mistaken —that recalled her from her dreams.

"I simply don't understand all this Thea business," a man's voice was saying; she recognized him as one of the boys from the Archives Section—Noah's Ark Cubs they were always called by the others, "but do exactly what you like."

And then it was Stephanie's voice that replied, "But naturally, Nigel, you know that I always do."

Thea stood up so that they should see her before more could be said; it was one of the primary rules of conduct that her mother had instilled into her. Stephanie's lips parted for a second in surprise, then, "Oh, Thea," she said, "I was coming to look for you. Nigel's asked us to go to their section dance. I said I had no idea what you'd arranged. . . ."

"But, of course, you must go," cried Thea, she felt sure that her lips looked blue with the cold.

"But is it what *you* would like, darling?" asked Stephanie.

"Oh, *I* shouldn't be able to go, I'm afraid, you see I told Mrs. Reynolds. . . ." Thea seemed to remember vaguely that this whole conversation had taken place many times before, could anticipate the disappointment and anger that burnt her as though it was a scene she had been rehearsing all her life.

"Oh, well, of course we can't come then, Nigel," Stephanie said hurriedly, and when the young man murmured something about promises, she added sharply,

"Don't be absurd, Nigel, you know I never make promises."

"Please, Stephanie," said Thea, "I'm sure you'd enjoy it much more. It'll only be a Christmas dinner at the billet, I'm afraid it'll be very boring."

Stephanie raised her eyebrows slightly and her voice was faintly disgusted, as she answered, "My dear, as if everything here wasn't boring. See you to-morrow, Nigel," she added in dismissal. She was clearly anxious that he should not witness Thea's emotion further. They stood for a moment silent after Nigel had gone.

"You *would* have liked to have gone..." began Thea, when Stephanie interrupted quite angrily, "Good Heaven's, I'm perfectly indifferent what I do," she cried; a moment later, she laughed rather shrilly, "I'm sorry," she said, "I'm afraid I'm not very good at all this. You see, it never occurs to me to think of anything that happens here as being important," and she disappeared into the house.

After a little Thea crept back to the shadow of the building. She stood for a moment, leaning against the brick wall, deliberately feeling its harsh surface through her costume, controlling a violent impulse to run after Stephanie and beg her assurance that the whole conversation had been an illusion, had never taken place, had been a joke. . . . Then, carefully shaping her mouth with her lipstick, she returned to the party.

Already beer drinking had begun and the carol singers were giving way to Tim and the "gang." A gramophone was playing "Paper Doll," "I'd rather have a paper doll to call my own" the crooner sang "than a fickle-minded real live doll." Thea accepted a strong gin, coughed at the first mouthful, and then with set expression, joined the little group surrounding Tim and his girl-friend.

"Cry-baby all right now?" the girl friend asked, and "Yes," answered Thea "Cry-baby's all right."

"My God! I don't know what they expect" said Tim.

"No" replied Thea, "you don't, Tim, you don't know what they expect."

"So that's for you, Tim" said one of the group.

"Oh, Thea and I understand each other don't we Thea?" said Tim, and "Oh yes, we understand each other, Tim" Thea said. She felt sure this was the right manner—bitter, quick, hard—it brought back something she had read in Hemingway, and the loud noise of the gramophone seemed to clinch the scene. In reality she didn't feel at all bitter, only humiliated and unhappy.

"Well" said Tim "here's to next Christmas, and the one after!"

"Think we'll be here, Tim?" asked a young lieutenant.

"Shouldn't be surprised" said Tim, "got 'em on the run, now, you know, and we've got to paste the bastards until they've forgotten *how* to squeal. Besides there's always the Nips." Two drinks always made him talk in this saloon bar manner, unless one of his superiors was about, when he tried to preserve some of his hard won gentlemanly behaviour.

"Two years from now, you'll be Deputy Director, Tim, and won't that be nice," Thea said. She had taken another drink and was prepared to say anything if only they would like her.

"She's got you there, Tim," they cried, and Tim said, "Touché. But honestly, Thea, you know as well as I do we can't let up now," he looked serious.

Thea, too, looked grave "I know, Tim," she said simply, though she wasn't quite sure to what he referred.

"Well, when you two have settled all our fates," said the girl friend, "we've got to move, darling."

Thea was amused to see that the girl was slightly jealous, so she smiled at Tim quizzically. Strangely enough he didn't respond, but followed his girl friend. Thea was puzzled, her memory of scenes on the films had been different from this.

Suddenly everyone moved off, and Thea found herself isolated again. She felt so unhappy that she could hardly restrain her tears. She had worked up a special vulgar manner, and there she was left with it on her hands. Suddenly she saw Stephanie coming towards her, and desperately she made for where Joan Fowler stood.

"Oh! Joan, we ought to be going," she cried, "I told my billet eight o'clock sharp and I've ordered a special car."

Joan Fowler looked bemused, but in a mist of happiness.

"Oh! Thea, I didn't remember. I *did* say to Penelope . . . oh! but it'll be quite alright. Shall I get my coat?" she cried.

Thea turned to Stephanie, "Oh my dear" she said,

drawling, "It's too awful of me.   I quite forgot last night, when I asked you, that Joan was coming.   I was half asleep, I think.   I'm afraid I daren't spring an unexpected guest on poor Mrs. Owens, our's is such a *very* humble home.   But you won't have missed anything, I'm sure you'd have found it an *awful* bore."

Totentanz

THE news of the Cappers' good fortune first became generally known at the Master's garden party. It was surprisingly well received, in view of the number of their enemies in the University, and for this the unusually fine weather was largely responsible. In their sub-arctic isolation, cut off from the main stream of Anglo-Saxon culture and its preferments, sodden with continual mists, pinched by perpetual north-east gales, kept always a little at bay by the natives with their self-satisfied homeliness and their smugly traditional hospitality, the dons and their wives formed a phalanx against spontaneous gaiety that would have satisfied John Knox himself. But rare though days of sunshine were, they transformed the town as completely as if it had been one of those scenes in a child's painting book on which you had only to sprinkle water for the brighter colours to emerge. The Master's lawns, surfeited with rain and mist, lay in flaunting spring green beneath the even deep blue of the July sky. The neat squares of the eighteenth-century burghers' houses and the twisted shapes of the massive grey loch-side ruins recovered their designs from the blurring mists. The clumps of wallflowers, gold and copper, filling the crevices of the walls, seemed to mock the solemnity of the covenanting crows that croaked censoriously above them. The famous pale blue silk of the scholars' gowns flashed like silver airships beneath the deeper sky. On such a day

even the most mildewed and disappointed of the pro-
fessors, the most blue and deadening of their wives felt
impulses of generosity, or at any rate a freedom from
bitterness, that allowed them to rejoice at a fellow-
prisoner's release. Only the youngest and most naive
research students could be deceived by the sun into
brushing the mould off their *own* hopes and ideals, but
if others had found a way back to their aims, well, good
luck to them!—in any case the Cappers, especially Mrs.
Capper, had only disturbed the general morass with
their futile struggles, most people would be glad to see
them go.

The Master's wife, always so eccentric in her large
fringed cape, said in her deep voice, "It's come just in
time. Just in time that is for Isobel."

"Just in time," squeaked little Miss Thurkill, the
assistant French lecturer, "I should have thought any
time was right for a great legacy like that," and she
giggled, really the old woman said such odd, personal
things.

"Yes, just in time," repeated the Master's wife, she
prided herself on understanding human beings and lost
no opportunity of expounding them. "A few months
more and she would have rotted away."

In the wide opening between the points of his old-
fashioned, high Gladstone collar, the Master's protrusive
Adam's apple wobbled, gulped. In Oxford or Cambridge
his wife's eccentricity would have been an assistance,
up here, had he not known exactly how to isolate her,
it might have been an embarrassment.

"How typical of women," he said in the unctuous

but incisive voice that convinced so many businessmen
and baillies that they were dealing with a scholar whose
head was screwed on the right way. "How typical of
women to consider only the legacy. Very nice of course,
a great help in their new sphere." There was a trace
of bitterness, for his own wife's fortune, so important
when they started, had vanished through his unfortunate
investments. "But Cappers' London Chair is the important thing. A new chair, too, Professory of the
History of Technics and Art. Here, of course, we've
come to accept so many of Capper's ideas into our
everyday thoughts, as a result of his immense powers of
persuasion and . . . and his great enthusiasm," he paused,
staring eagle-like beneath his bushy white eyebrows, the
scholar who was judge of men, "that we forget how rev-
olutionary some of them are," he had indeed the vaguest
conception of anything that his subordinates thought,
an administrator has to keep above detail. "No doubt
there'll be fireworks, but I venture to suggest that
Capper's youth and energy will win the day, don't you
agree with me, Todhurst?"

Mr. Todhurst's white suet pudding face tufted with
sandy hair was unimpressed. He was a great deal younger
than Capper and still determined to remember what a
backwater he was stranded in. "Capper's noot so
young," he said, ostentatiously Yorkshire. "Maybe
they'll have heard it all before, and happen they'll tell
him so too."

But the Master was conveniently able to ignore
Todhurst for red-faced Sir George was approaching,
the wealthiest, most influential businessman on the

University Board. A tough and rough diamond with his Glaswegian accent and his powerful whiskied breath, Sir George was nevertheless impressed by the size of the legacy. "Five hundred thousand pounds." He gave a whistle. "That's no so bad a sum. Though, mind you, this Government of robbers'll be taking a tidy part of it away in taxation. But still I'm glad for the sake of his missus." Perhaps, he thought, Mrs. Capper would help in getting Margaret presented at Court. How little he knew Isobel Capper; his wife would not have made the mistake.

"And this magnificent appointment coming along at the same time," said the Master.

"Aye," said Sir George, he did not understand that so well, "there's no doubt Capper's a smart young chap." Perhaps, he thought, the Board has been a bit slow, the Master was getting on and they might need a level-headed warm young fellow.

"Oh, there they are," squeaked Miss Thurkill excitedly, "I must say Isobel certainly looks . . ." but she could find no words to describe Isobel's appearance, it was really so very outrée.

Nothing could have fitted Isobel Capper's combination of chic and Liberty artiness better than the ultra-smart dressing-gown effect of her New Look dress, the floating flimsiness of her little flowered hat. Her long stride was increased with excitement, even her thin white face had relaxed its tenseness and her amber eyes sparkled with triumph. Against the broad pink and black stripes of her elaborate, bustled dress, her red hair clashed like fire. She was a little impatient with the tail-end of an

episode that she was glad to close, her mind was crowded
with schemes, but still this victory parade, though petty
and provincial, would be a pleasant start to a new life.
Brian, too, looked nearer twenty than forty, most of his
hard, boyish charm, his emphasized friendliness and
sincerity had returned with the prospect of his new
appointment. He tossed his brown curly hair back from
his forehead, as loose limbed, athletic, he leaped a deck
chair to speak to Sir George. "Hope so very much to
see something of you and Lady Maclean if all those
company meetings permit." Before the Master he stood
erect, serious, a little abashed. "So impossible to speak
adequately of what I shall carry away from here. . . ."
There was no doubt that Brian was quite himself again.
His even white teeth gleamed as he smiled at the Master's
wife. To her he presented himself almost with a wink
as the professional charmer, because after all she was
not a woman you could fool. "The awful thing is that my
first thought about it is for all the fun we're going to
have." With Todhurst he shared their contempt for
the backwater. "Not going to say I wish you'd got the
appointment, because I don't. Besides kunstgeschichte,
old man! you and I know what a bloody fraud the whole
thing is. Not that I don't intend to make something
useful out of it all, and that's exactly why I've got to
pick your brains before I go south." It was really
amazing, Isobel thought, how the news had revived
him—alive, so terribly keen and yet modest withal,
and behind everything steady as a rock, a young chap
of forty, in fact, who would go far.

Her own method was far more direct, she had never

shared her husband's spontaneous sense of salesman-
ship, at times even found it nauseating. There was no
need to bother about these people any more and she
did not intend to do so. "Silly to say we shall meet again,
Sir George," she told him, before he could get round
to asking. "It's only in the bonny north that the arts
are conducted on purely business lines." Todhurst,
like all the other junior dons, she ignored. "You must
be so happy," said Jessie Colquhoun, the poetess of the
lochs. "I shan't be *quite* happy," Isobel replied, "until
we've crossed the Border." "Of *course* we shall lose
touch," she said to the Master's wife, "but I'm not so
pleased as you think I am." And really, she thought,
if the old woman's eccentricity had not been quite so
provincial and frowsty it might have been possible
to invite her to London. Her especial venom was
reserved for the Master himself. "Dear Mrs. Capper,"
he intoned. "What a tremendous loss you will be to us,
and Capper, too, the ablest man on the Faculty." "I
wonder what you'll say to the Board when they wake
up to their loss, as I'm sure they will," replied Isobel.
"It'll take a lot of explaining."

And yet the Master's wife was quite right, it was only
just in time for both of them. Brian had begun to slip
back badly in the last few years. His smile, the very centre
of his charm, had grown too mechanical, gum recession
was giving him an equine look. His self-satisfaction
which had once made him so friendly to all—useful
and useless alike—had begun to appear as heavy indifference. When he had first come north he had danced
like a shadow-boxer from one group to another, making

the powerful heady with praise, giving to the embittered a cherished moment of flattery, yet never committing himself; engaging all hearts by his youthful belief in Utopia, so much more acceptable because he was obviously so fundamentally sound. But with the years his smiling sincerity had begun to change to dogmatism; he could afford his own views and often they were not interesting, occasionally very dull. Younger colleagues annoyed him, he knew that they thought him out of date. Though he still wanted always to be liked, he had remained "a young man" too long to have any technique for charming the *really* young. Faced by their contempt, he was often rude and sulky. The long apprenticeship in pleasing—the endless years of scholarships and examinations, of being the outstanding student of the year—were now too far behind to guard him from the warping atmosphere of the town. Commonwealths and Harmsworths were becoming remote memories, the Dulwich trams of his schooldays, the laurel bushes of his suburban childhood were closer to him now than the dreams and ambitions of Harvard, Oxford and Macgill. Had the chair come a year later he would probably have refused it. He had been such a success at thirty-three, it would have been easy to forget that at forty he was no longer an infant phenomenon.

If Brian had been rescued from the waters of Lethe in the nick of time, Isobel had been torn from the flames of hell. Her hatred of the University and the heat of her ambition had begun to burn her from within, until the strained, white face with cheekbones almost bursting through the skin and the over-intense eyes recalled some

witch in death agonies. It did not take long for the
superiority of her wit and taste to cease to bother a
world in which they were unintelligible, depression and
a lack of audience soon gave her irony a "governessy"
flavour, until at last the legend of Mrs. Capper's sharp
tongue had begun to bore herself as much as others.
The gold and white satin, the wooden negro page of
her Regency room had begun to fret her nerves with
their shabbiness, yet it seemed pointless to furnish
anew, even if she could have afforded it, for a world
she so much despised. She made less and less pretence
of reading or listening to music, and yet for months
she would hardly stir outside. Everything that might
have been successful in a more sophisticated society
was misunderstood here: her intellectual Anglicanism
was regarded as dowdy churchgoing, her beloved
Caravaggio was confused with Greuze, her Purcell
enthusiasm thought to be a hangover from the time
when the "Beggar's Opera" was all the rage; she would
have done far better, been thought more daring with
Medici van Goghs and some records of the Bolero.
She had come to watch all Brian's habits with horror,
his little provincial don's sarcasms, his tobacco-jarred,
golfy homeliness, his habit of pointing with his pipe
and saying: "Now hold on a minute I want to examine
this average man or woman of yours more carefully";
or "Anarchism, now, that's a very interesting word,
but are we *quite* sure we know what it means?" She
became steadily more afraid of "going to pieces,"
knew herself to be toppling on the edge of a neurotic
apathy from which she would never recover.

It was not surprising therefore that as she said good-
bye for the third time to old Professor Green who was
so absent-minded, she blessed the waves that had sucked
Aunt Gladys down in a confusion of flannel petticoats
and straggling grey hair, or the realistic sailor who had
cut Uncle Joseph's bony fingers from the side of an
overloaded lifeboat. She was rich, rich enough to realize
her wildest ambitions; beside this Brian's professorship
seemed of little importance. And yet in Isobel's growing
schemes it had its place, for she had determined to storm
London and she was quite shrewd enough to realize
that she would never take that citadel by force of cash
alone, far better to enter by the academic gate she knew
so well.

By January six months of thick white mists and driving
rain had finally dissipated the faint traces of July's
charity, and with them all interest in the Cappers'
fortunes. The Master's wife, dragged along by her two
French bulldogs, was fighting her way through Aidan's
arch against a battery of hail when she all but collided
with Miss Thurkill returning from lunch at the British
Restaurant. She would have passed on with a nod but Miss
Thurkill's red fox-terrier nose was quivering with news.

"The Cappers' good fortune seems to have been
quite a sell," she yelped. "They've got that great house
of her uncle's on their hands."

"From all I hear about London conditions Penton-
ville Prison would be a prize these days," boomed the
Master's wife.

"Oh, but that isn't all. It's quite grisly," giggled Miss Thurkill. "They've got to have the bodies in the house for ever and ever. It's part of the conditions of the will."

Boredom had given the Master's wife a conviction of psychic as well as psychological powers and she suddenly "felt aware of evil."

"I was wrong when I said that silly little woman was saved in time. Pathetic creature with her cheap ambitions and her dressing-up clothes, she's in for a very bad time."

Something of the old woman's prophetic mood was communicated to Miss Thurkill and she found herself saying:

"I know. Isn't it horrible?"

For a moment they stood outlined against the grey stormy sky, the Master's wife, her great black mackintosh cape billowing out behind, like an evil bat, Miss Thurkill sharp and thin like a barking jackal. Then the younger woman laughed nervously.

"Well, I must rush on or I'll be drenched to the skin."

She could not hear the other's reply for the howling of the wind, but it sounded curiously like "Why not?"

Miss Thurkill was, of course, exaggerating wildly when she spoke of "bodies" in the house, because the bones of Uncle Joseph and Aunt Gladys were long since irrevocably Atlantic coral or on the way to it. But there was a clause in the will that was troublesome enough to give Isobel great cause for anxiety in the midst of her triumphant campaign for power.

A very short time had been needed to prove that the Cappers were well on the way to a brilliant success. Todhurst had proved a false prophet, Brian had been received with acclamations in the London academic world, not only within the University, but in the smart society of the Museums and Art Galleries, and in the houses of rich connoisseurs, art dealers, smart sociologists and archaeologists with chic, that lay around its periphery. It has to be remembered that many of those with Brian's peculiar brand of juvenile careerist charm were now getting a little passé and tired, whilst the post-war generation were somehow too total in outlook, too sure of their views to achieve the necessary flexibility, the required chameleon character. Brian might have passed unnoticed in 1935, in 1949 he appeared as a refreshing draught from the barbaric north. Already his name carried weight at the high tables of All Souls and King's—a man to watch. He talked on the Third Programme and on the Brains Trust—Isobel was a bit doubtful about this—he reviewed for smart weeklies and monthlies, he was commissioned to write a Pelican book.

Isobel was pleased with all this, but she aimed at something more than an academical sphere however chic—she was incurably romantic and over Brian's shoulder she saw a long line of soldier-mystics back from Persia, introvert explorers, able young Conservatives, important Dominicans, and Continental novelists with international reputations snatched from the jaws of O.G.P.U. —and at the centre, herself, the woman who counted. Brian's success would be a help, their money more so.

For the moment her own role was a passive one, she was content if she "went down," and for this her chic Anglo-Catholicism—almost Dominican in theological flavour, almost Jesuit Counter Reformation in aesthetic taste—combined with her spiteful wit, power of mimicry and interesting appearance, sufficed. Meanwhile she was watching and learning, entertaining lavishly, being pleasant to everyone and selecting carefully the important few who were to carry them on to the next stage—the most influential people within their present circle, but not, and here she was most careful, people who were too many jumps ahead; they would come later. By the time that this ridiculous, this insane clause in the will had been definitely proven, she had already chosen the four people who must be cultivated.

First and most obviously, Professor Cadaver, that long gaunt old man with his corseted figure, his military moustache and his almost too beautiful clothes; foremost of archaeologists, author of "Digging up the Dead", "The Tomb my Treasurehouse" and "Where Grave thy Victory?" It was not only the tombs of the ancient world on which he was a final authority, for in the intervals between his expeditions to the Near East and North Africa, he had familiarized himself with all the principal cemeteries of the British Isles and had formed a remarkable collection of photographs of unusual graves. His enthusiasm for the ornate masonry of the nineteenth century had given him *réclame* among the devotees of Victorian art. He enthusiastically supported Brian's views on the sociological importance of burial customs, though he often irritated his younger colleague by the

emphasis he seemed to lay upon the state of preservation
of the bodies themselves. Over embalming in particular
he would wax very enthusiastic—"Every feature, every
limb preserved in their lifetime beauty," he would say,
"and yet over all the odour of decay, the sweet stillness of
death." A strange old man! For Isobel, too, he seemed
to have a great admiration, he would watch her with his
old reptilian eyes for hours on end—"What wonderful
bone-structure," he would say; "One can almost *see* the
cheek bones." "How few people one sees to-day, Mrs.
Capper, with your perfect pallor, at times it seems almost
livid."

Over Lady Maude she hesitated longer, there were so
many old women—well-connected and rich—who were
interested in art history and of these Lady Maude was
physically the least prepossessing. With her little myopic
pig's eyes, her wide-brimmed hats insecurely pinned to
falling coils of hennaed hair and her enormous body en-
cased in musquash she might have been passed over by
any eye less sharp than Isobel's. But Lady Maude had
been everywhere and seen everything. Treasures locked
from all other Western gaze by Soviet secrecy or Muslim
piety had been revealed to her. American millionaires
had shown her masterpieces of provenance so dubious
that they could not be publicly announced without international complications. She had spent many hours
watching the best modern fakers at work. Her memory
was detailed and exact, and although her eyesight was
failing, her strong glasses still registered what she saw as
though it had been photographed by the camera. Outside
her knowledge of the arts she was intensely stupid and

thought only of her food. This passionate greed she tried to conceal, but Isobel soon discovered it, and set out to win her with every delicacy that the Black Market could provide.

With Taste and Scholarship thus secured, Isobel began to cast about for a prop outside the smart academic world, a stake embedded deep in café society. The thorns that surrounded the legacy were beginning to prick. She still refused to believe that the fantastic, the wicked clause, could really be valid and had set all London's lawyers to refute it. But even so there were snags. It was necessary, for example, that they should leave the large furnished flat which they had taken in Cadogan Street and occupy Uncle Joseph's rambling mansion in Portman Square, with its mass of miscellaneous middle-class junk assembled since 1890; so much the will made perfectly clear. The district, she felt, might do. But before the prospect of filling the house, and filling it correctly, with furniture, servants, and above all, guests, she faltered. It was at this moment that she met Guy Rice. Since coming to London she had seen so many beautiful pansy young men, all with the same standard voices, jargon, bow-ties and compli- cated hair-do's, that she tended now to ignore them. That some of them were important, she felt no doubt, but it was difficult to distinguish amid such uniformity and she did not wish to make a mistake. Guy Rice, however, decided to know *her*. He sensed at once her insecurity, her hardness and her determination. She was just the wealthy peg he needed on which to hang his great flair for pastiche, which he saw with alarm was in danger of becoming a drug on the market. Mutual robbery, after all, was fair exchange, he thought, as he watched her talking to a little group before the fire.

"I can never understand," she was saying, "why people who've made a mess of things should excuse themselves by saying that they can't accept authority. But then *I* don't think insanity's a very good plea." It was one of her favourite themes. Guy patted the couch beside him.

"Come and sit here, dearie," he said in the flat cockney whine he had always refused to lose—it was, after all, a distinction.

"You *do* try hard, dear, don't you? But you know it won't do." And then he proceeded to lecture and advise her on how to behave. Amazingly, Isobel did not find herself at all annoyed. As he said, "You could be so cosy, dear, if you tried, and that would be nice, wouldn't it? All this clever talk's very well, but what people want is a good old-fashioned bit of fun. What they want is parties, great big slap-up do's like we had in the old days," for Guy was a rather old young man. "Lots of fun, childish, you know, elaborate and a wee bit nasty; and you're just the girl to give it to them." He looked closely at her emaciated, white face. "The skeleton at the feast, dear, that's you."

Their rather surprising friendship grew daily—shopping, lunching, but mostly just sitting together over a cup of tea, for they both dearly loved a good gossip. He put her wise about everyone, hard-boiled estimates with a dash of good scout sentimentality—it was "I shouldn't see too much of them, dear, they're on the out. Poor old dears! They say they were ever such naughties once," or "Cling on for dear life. She's useful. Let her talk, duckie, that's the thing. She likes it. Gets a bit lonely sometimes, I expect, like we all do." He reassured her, too, about her husband.

"What do you think of Brian?" she had asked.

"Same as you do, dear. He bores me dizzy. But don't you worry, there's thousands love that sort of thing. Takes all sorts to make a world."

He put her clothes right for her, saying with a sigh, "Oh, Isobel, dear, you *do* look tatty," until she left behind that touch of outré artiness that the Master's wife had been so quick to see. With his help she made a magnificent if somewhat over-perfect, spectacle of the Portman Square Mansion. His knowledge of interior decoration was very professional and with enough money and rooms he let his love of pastiche run wild. He was wise enough to leave the show pieces—the Zurbaran, the Fragonard, the Samuel Palmers and the Bracques to the Professor and Lady Maude—but for the rest he just let rip. There were Regency bedrooms, a Spanish Baroque dining room, a Second Empire room, a Victorian study, something amusing in Art Nouveau; but his greatest triumph of all was a large lavatory with tubular furniture, American cloth and cacti in pots. "Let's have a dear old pre-war lav. in the nice old-fashioned Munich style," he had said and the Cappers, wondering, agreed.

On one point only did they differ, Isobel was adamant in favour of doing things as economically as possible, both she and Brian had an innate taste for saving. With this aspect of her life Guy refused to be concerned, but he introduced her to her fourth great prop—Tanya Mule.

"She's the biggest bitch unhung, duckie," he said, "but she'll touch propositions no one else will. She's had it all her own way ever since the war, when 'fiddling' began in a big way."

Mrs. Mule had been very beautiful in the style of Gladys Cooper, but now her face was ravaged into a million lines and wrinkles from which two large and deep blue eyes stared in dead appeal; she wore her hair piled up very high and coloured very purple; she always dressed in the smartest black of Knightsbridge with a collar of pearls. She was of the greatest help to Isobel, for although she charged a high commission, she knew every illegal avenue for getting servants and furniture and decorator's men and unrationed food; she could smell out bankruptcy over miles of territory and was always first at the sale; she knew every owner of objets d'art who was in distress and exactly how little they could be made to take. No wonder, then, that with four such allies Isobel felt sure of her campaign.

Suddenly, however, in the flush of victory the great blow struck her—the lawyers decided that the wicked, criminal lunatic clause in Uncle Joseph's will must stand. Even Brian was forced up from beneath his life of lectures, and talks, and dinners to admit that the crisis was serious. Isobel was in despair. She looked at the still unfurnished drawing room—they had decided on Louis Treize—and thought of the horrors that must be perpetrated there. Certainly the issue was too big to be decided alone, they must call a council of their allies.

Isobel paced up and down in front of the great open fire as she talked, pulling her cigarette out of her tautened mouth and blowing quick angry puffs of smoke. She looked now at the Zurbaran friar with his ape and his owl, now at the blue and buff tapestried huntsmen who rode among the fleshy nymphs and satyrs, occasionally she glanced at Guy as he lay sprawled on the floor, twirling a Christmas rose, but never at Brian, or Lady Maude, Mrs. Mule or the Professor as they sat upright on their high-backed tapestried chairs. "I had hoped never to have to tell you," she said. "Of course, it's absolutely clear that Uncle Joseph and Aunt Gladys were completely insane at the time when the will was made, but apparently the law doesn't care about that. Oh! it's so typical of a country where sentimentalism reigns supreme without regard for God's authority or even for the Natural law for that matter. A crazy, useless old couple, steeped in some nonconformist nonsense, decide on an act of tyrannous interference with the future and all the lawyers can talk about is the liberty of an Englishman to dispose of his money as he wishes. Just because of that, the whole of our lives—Brian's and mine—are to be ruined, we're to be made a laughing stock. Just listen to this: 'If the Great Harvester should see fit to gather my dear wife and me to Him when we are on the high seas or in any other manner by which our mortal remains may not be recovered for proper Christian burial and in places where our dear niece and nephew, or under God, other heirs may decently commune with us and in other approved ways show us their respect and affection, then I direct that two memorials, which I have already caused to be made, shall be set in that room in our house in Portman Square in which they entertain their friends, that we may in some way share, assist and participate in their happy pastimes. This is absolutely to be carried out, so that if they shall not agree the whole of our estate shall pass to the charities hereinafter named.' And that" Isobel cried. "*that* is what the law says we shall have to do." She paused, dramatically waving the document in the air. "Well," said Guy, "I'm not partial to monuments myself, but they can be very nice, Isobel dear." "Nice," cried Isobel, "nice. Come and look;" and she threw open the great double doors into the drawing-room. The little party followed her solemnly.

It was perfectly true that the monuments could not be called nice. In the first place they were each seven feet high. Then they were made in white marble—not solid mid-Victorian, something could have been done with that, nor baroque, with angels and gold trumpets, which would have been better still, they were in the most exaggeratedly simple modern good taste by an amateur craftsman, a long way after Eric Gill. "My dear," said Guy, "they're horrors"; and Lady Maude remarked that they were not the kind of thing one ever wanted to see. The lettering, too, was bold, modern and very artful— one read "Joseph Briggs. Ready at the call." and the other "Gladys Briggs. Steel true, blade straight, the Great Artificer made my mate." Professor Cadaver was most distressed by them, "Really, without *any*thing in them," he kept on saying. "Nothing, not even ashes. It all seems most unfortunate." He appeared to feel that a great opportunity had been missed. No one had any suggestion to make. Mrs. Mule knew the names of many crooked lawyers and even a criminal undertaker, but this

did not seem to be quite in their line. Lady Maude
privately thought that as long as the dining room and
kitchen could function there was really very little reason
for anxiety. They all stood about in gloom, when suddenly Guy cried, "What did you say the lawyers were
called?" "Robertson, Naismith and White," said Isobel,
"but it's no good, we've gone over all that." "Trust
little Guy, dear," said her friend. Soon his voice could
be heard excitedly talking over the telephone. He was
there for more than twenty minutes, they could hear little
of what he said, though once he screamed rather angrily
"Never said I did say I did say I did," and at least twice
he cried petulantly "Aow, pooh!" When he returned he
put his hand on Isobel's shoulder. "It's all right, ducks,"
he said. "I've fixed it. Now we can all be cosy and that's
nice, isn't it?" Sitting tailor-wise on the floor, he produced
his solution with reasonable pride. "You see," he said,
"it only says in the will 'set in that room in which they
entertain their friends.' But it doesn't say you need entertain with those great horrors in the room more than
once and after a great deal of tiresome talk those lawyers
have agreed that I'm right. For that one entertainment
we'll build our setting round the horrors, Isobel dear,
everything morbid and ghostly. Your first big reception,
duckie, shall be a Totentanz. It's just the sort of special
send off you need. After that, pack the beastly things off,
and Presto, dear, back to normal."

The Totentanz was Isobel's greatest, alas! her last,
triumph. The vast room was swathed in black and

purple, against which the huge white monuments and other smaller tombstones specially designed for the occasion stood out in bold relief. The waiters and barmen were dressed as white skeletons or elaborate Victorian mutes with black ostrich plumes. The open fire place was arranged as a crematorium fire, and the chairs and tables were coffins made in various woods. Musical archives had been ransacked for funeral music of every age and clime. A famous Jewish contralto wailed like the ghetto, an African beat the tomtom as it is played at human sacrifices, an Irish tenor made everyone weep with his wake songs. Supper was announced by "The Last Post" on a bugle and hearses were provided to carry the guests home.

Some of the costumes were most original. Mrs. Mule came tritely but aptly enough as a Vampire. Lady Maude with her hair screwed up in a handkerchief and dressed in a shapeless gown was strikingly successful as Marie Antoinette shaved for the guillotine. Professor Cadaver dressed up as a Corpse Eater was as good as Boris Karloff; he clearly enjoyed every minute of the party, indeed his snake-like slit eyes darted in every direction at the many beautiful young women dressed as corpses and his manner became so incoherent and excited before he left that Isobel felt quite afraid to let him go home alone. Guy had thought at first of coming as Millais's Ophelia, but he remembered the harm done to the original model's health and decided against it. With flowing hair and marbled features, however, he made a very handsome "Suicide of Chatterton." Isobel thought he seemed a little melancholy during the evening, but when she asked him if anything was wrong he replied quite absently, "No, dear, nothing really. Half in love with easeful death, I 'spose. I mean all this fun *is* rather hell when it comes to the point, isn't it?" But when he saw her face cloud, he said, "Don't you worry, ducks, you've arrived," and, in fact, Isobel, was too happy to think of anyone but herself. For many hours after the last guests had departed, she sat happily chipping away at the monuments with a hammer. She sang a little to herself: "I've beaten you, Uncle and Auntie dear, I hope it's the last you'll bother us here."

Guy felt very old and weary as he let himself into his one-roomed luxury flat. He realized that Isobel would not be needing him much longer, soon she would be on the way to spheres beyond his ken. There were so many really young men who could do his stuff now and they didn't get bored or tired in the middle like he did. Suddenly he saw a letter in the familiar, uneducated handwriting lying on the mat. He turned giddy for a moment and leaned against the wall. It would be impossible to go on finding money like this for ever. Perhaps this time he could get it from Isobel, after all she owed most of her success to him, but it would hasten the inevitable break with her. And even if he had the courage to settle this, there were so many more demands in different uneducated hands, so much more past sentimentalism turned to fear. He lay for a long time in the deep green bath, then sat in front of his double mirror to perform a complicated routine with creams and powders. At last he put on a crimson and white silk dressing gown and hung his

Chatterton wig and costume in the wardrobe. He wished
so much that Chatterton were there to talk to. Then
going to the white painted medicine cupboard, he took
out his bottle of luminal. "In times like these," he said
aloud, "there's nothing like a good old overdose to pull
one through."

Lady Maude enjoyed the party immensely. The funeral
baked meats were delicious and Isobel had seen that the
old lady had all she wanted. She sat on the edge of her
great double bed, with her grey hair straggling about her
shoulders, and swung her thick white feet with their
knobbly blue veins. The caviare and chicken mayonnaise
and Omelette Surprise lay heavy upon her, but she found,
as usual, that indigestion only made her the more hungry.
Suddenly she remembered the game pie in the larder. She
put on her ancient padded pink dressing gown and tiptoed
downstairs—it would not do for the Danbys to hear her,
servants could make one look so foolish. But when she
opened the larder, she was horrified to find that someone
had forestalled her, the delicious, rich game pie had been
removed. The poor, cheated lady was not long in finding
the thief. She padded into the kitchen and there, seated
at the table, noisily guzzling the pie, was a very young
man with long fair hair, a red and blue checked shirt and
a white silk tie with girls in scarlet bathing costumes on it;
he looked as though he suffered from adenoids. Lady
Maude had read a good deal in her favourite newspapers
about spivs and burglars so that she was not greatly
surprised. Had he been in the act of removing the silver,
she would have fled in alarm, but as it was she felt nothing
but anger. Her whole social foundation seemed to shake

beneath the wanton looting of her favourite food. She immediately rushed towards him, shouting for help The man—he was little more than a youth and very frightened —struck at her wildly with a heavy iron bar. Lady Maude fell backwards upon the table, almost unconscious and bleeding profusely. Then the boy completely lost his head and, seizing up the kitchen meat axe, with a few wild strokes he severed her head from her body. She died like a queen.

Only the moon lit the vast spaces of Brompton Cemetery, showing up here a tomb and there a yew tree. Professor Cadaver's eyes were wild and his hands shook as he glided down the central pathway. His head still whirled with the fumes of the party and a thousand beautiful corpses danced before his eyes. An early Underground train rattled in the distance and he hurried his steps. At last he reached his objective—a freshly dug grave on which wooden planks and dying wreaths were piled. The Professor began feverishly to tear these away, but he was getting old and neither his sight nor his step were as sure as they had been, he caught his foot in a rope and fell nine or ten feet into the tomb. When they found him in the morning his neck was broken. The papers hushed up the affair, and a Sunday newspaper in an article entitled "Has Science the Right?" only confused the matter by describing him as a professor of anatomy and talking obscurely of Burke and Hare.

It was the end of Isobel's hopes. True, Mrs. Mule still remained to play the vampire, but without the others she was as nothing. Indeed, the position for Isobel was worse than when she arrived in London, for it would take a long time to live down her close association with the Professor and Guy.   Brian was a little nonplussed at first, but there was so much to do at the University, that he had little time to think of what might have been. He was now the centre of a circle of students and lecturers who listened to his every word. As Isobel's social schemes faded, he began to fill the house with his friends. Sometimes she would find him standing full square before the Zurbaran pointing the end of his pipe at a party of earnest young men sitting bolt upright on the tapestried chairs. "Ah," he would be saying jocosely, "but you haven't yet proved to me that your famous average man or woman is anything but a fiction," or "But look here, Wotherspoon, you can't just throw words like 'beauty' or 'formal design' about like that.   We must define our terms." Once she discovered a tobacco pouch and a Dorothy Sayers' detective novel on a tubular chair in the "dear old lav." But if Brian had turned the house into a W.E.A. lecture centre, Isobel would not have protested now. Her thoughts were too much with the dead. She sat all day in the vast empty drawing room, where the two great monuments threw their giant shadows over her.   Here she would smoke an endless chain of cigarettes and drink tea off unopened packing cases. Occasionally she would glance up at the inscriptions with a look of mute appeal, but she never seemed to find an answer. She made less and less pretence of reading and listening to good music, and yet for months on end would hardly stir from the house.

A faint April sun shone down upon the wet pavements

of the High Street, casting a faint and melancholy light
upon the pools of rain that had gathered here and there
among the cobblestones. It was a deceptive gleam, however, for the wind was piercingly cold. Miss Thurkill
drew her B.A. gown tightly round her thin frame as she
emerged from the lecture hall and hurried off to the
Heather Café. Turning the corner by Strachan's book-
shop, she saw the Master's wife advancing upon her.
Despite the freezing weather, the old lady moved slowly,
for the bitter winter's crop of influenza and bronchitis
had weakened her heart; she seemed now as fat and wad-
dling as her bulldogs.

"Did you get the London appointment?" she shouted;
it was a cruel question, for she knew already the negative
reply. "Back to the tomb, eh?" she went on. "Ah well!
at least we know we're dead here."

Miss Thurkill giggled nervously; "London didn't seem
very alive," she said. "I went to see the Cappers, but I
couldn't get any reply. The whole house seemed to be
shut up."

"Got the plague, I expect," said the Master's wife,
"took it from here," and as she laughed to herself, she
crouched forward like some huge, squat toad.

"Isobel certainly hasn't been the success she supposed,"
hissed Miss Thurkill, writhing like a malicious snake.
"Well, I shall catch my death of cold if I stay here," she
added, and hurried on.

The old lady's voice came to her in the gale that blew
down the street: "No one would notice the difference,"
it seemed to cry.

Mummy to the Rescue

NURSE Ramsay was an incongruous figure in her friend Marjorie's dainty little room. Her muscular, almost masculine, arms and legs seemed to emerge uneasily from the cosy chintz-covered chair, her broad, thick-fingered hands moved cumbrously among the Venetian glass swans and crocheted silk table mats. To-night she seemed even more like an Amazon at rest. She was half asleep after a tiring and difficult day with her charge, yet the knowledge that she must get up from her hostess's cheerful fireside and make her way home along the deserted village street through torrents of rain and against a bitter gale forced her into painful, bad tempered wakefulness. Her huge brow was puckered with lines of resentment, her lips set tight with envy of her friend's independence. It was easy enough to be dainty and sweet if you had a place of your own, but a nurse's position—neither servant nor companion—was a very different matter. She bit almost savagely into the chocolate biscuits, arranged so prettily by Marjorie in the little silver dish, and her glass of warm lemonade seemed only to add to the sourness of her mood.

"Of course, if they weren't so wealthy," she said, "they'd have to send her away, granddaughter or no granddaughter. She's got completely out of hand."

"I suppose the old people like to have her with them," said Marjorie in her jolly, refined voice. She licked the chocolate from her fingers, each in turn, holding them out in a babyish, captivating way of which however, Nurse Ramsay was too cross to take any notice. "But she *does* sound a holy terror. Poor old Joey," for so she called Nurse Ramsay, "you must have a time with her. They've spoilt her, that's the trouble."

Nurse Ramsay drew her legs apart, and the heavy woollen skirt hitched above her knees, displaying the thick grey of her winter knickers, allowing a suspender to glint in the firelight.

"Spoilt," she said in her deep voice with its Australian twang. "I should think *so* if you *can* spoil a cracked pot. I've had many tiresome ones, but our dear Celia takes the biscuit. The tempers, the sulking you wouldn't believe, and violent, too, sometimes; of course she doesn't know her own strength. So selfish with her toys —that's Mrs. Hartley's fault, 'Whatever she wants, nurse,' she told me, 'we must give her, it's the least we can do.' Well! I ask you—of course the old lady's getting a bit queer herself, that's the trouble, and the old gentleman's not much better. 'You're asking for trouble,' I told her, but you might as well talk to a stone wall. You should have heard the fuss the other day just because I couldn't find an old doll. 'If other little girls bit and scratched when they lost their dolls,' I said."

Marjorie gave a little scream of laughter. Nurse Ramsay scowled, she was always suspicious of ridicule.

"What's funny about that?" she asked. "Oh nothing I s'pose," said Marjorie, "if you're used to it, but better you than me."

"I should think so," said Nurse Ramsay, "why

Doctor Lardner said to me only the other day, 'Nobody but you would stand it, Nurse, you must have nerves of steel.' I suppose I am unusually. . . ."

But Marjorie had closed her ears to a familiar story. She was busy wiping a chocolate stain from her pretty blue crepe-de-chine frock, liberally soaking her little lace-bordered hanky with spittle to perform the task. Really Joey was always full of moans nowadays.

It was so very dark in the little bed and if you turned one way you would fall out and if you turned the other it was wall and you were shut in. Celia held her doll very tightly to her. She was shaking all over with fright, Nanny had pushed and scratched so because she wanted Mummy in bed with her. Nanny always tried to stop her having Mummy, because she was jealous. But you had to be careful, you had to watch your time, because however much you bit, squelching and driving the teeth into the arm-flesh, cracking the bone, they could always tie you in, as they had done before, and then even Grannie didn't help you. So she had pretended to Nanny that she was beaten, that she would do without Mummy. But Nanny did not know Mummy was in bed. Celia pushed back the clothes and looked at the familiar blue wool by the light of the moonbeam from the window-shutter. "It's alright when Mummy's with you, darling," so long ago she had said that, before she went on the ship, leaving her with Granny. "I shall be back with you before you can say Jack Robinson," she had said, as Celia sat on the edge of the cabin trunk and wrapped her doll in the old blue cardigan. She did not come and she did not come and then she was there all the time in the blue cardigan and if she was with you it was alright. But you had to be very careful not to let them part you from Mummy's protection—they could do it by force, but only for a little because Granny wouldn't allow it; but the worst was when they tricked you into losing; Nanny had done that once and they had searched and searched, at least all of them had except Nanny, and she pretended to, but all the time you could tell from her eyes that she was wishing they would never find. The look in Nanny's eyes had enraged Celia and she had scratched until the blood ran. That had meant a bad time following, with Granny angry and Granddad's voice loud and stern, and being held into bed and little white pills. No, it was important never to be separated—so Celia took Mummy and very carefully passing the arms round her neck, she knotted them to the bedpost behind her. It was very difficult to do, but at last she was satisfied that Nanny could not separate them. Then she lay back and watched the yellow moonlight from the window. Yellow was the middle light, and as they drove behind Goddard in the car—Goddard who gave the barley-sugar—with Granny smelling of flowers, they would say yellow that was the middle light, and green we move, and red we must stop, and green we move, and yellow was the middle light, and red we stop. . . .

"It's simply a question of the money not being there," said old Mr. Hartley, and his voice was cracked and irritable. He didn't like the business any more than his wife, and yet her refusal to comprehend financial dealings —thirty-five years before he would have found it feminine, charming—was putting him into the role of advocate, of cruel realist. He had already succumbed to a glass of port in his agitation at the whole idea, and the thought of to-morrow's gout was a further irritant.

"Well, you know best, dear, of course," his wife answered in that calm, pacifying voice which had vexed him over so many years, "but you've often said we ought to change our lawyers, that Mr. Cartwright was a terrible old woman. . . ."

"Yes, yes, I know," Mr. Hartley broke in, "Cartwright's an old fool, but he isn't responsible for taxation and this damned government. The truth is, my dear, we're living on very diminished capital and we just can't afford it."

"Well I do my best to economize," said Mrs. Hartley, "but prices. . . ."

"I know, I know," Mr. Hartley broke in again, "but it isn't a question of cheeseparing here and there. We've got to change our whole way of living. In the first place we've got to find somewhere cheaper and smaller to live."

"Well, I don't know how you think we're all going to fit into a smaller house," said his wife.

"That's just the point," he replied, "I don't." He pulled his upper lip over the lower and stared into the fire, then he looked up at his wife as though he expected her to be waiting for him to say more. But she had no thought for his continuing, only a deep abhorrence and refusal of the proposal he had implied. She folded her embroidery and, getting up, she moved the pot of cyclamens from the little table by the window. "You've been letting Nurse Ramsay get at you," she said.

"Letting Nurse Ramsay get at me," echoed the old man savagely, "what nonsense you do talk, dear. Anyone would think I was a child who couldn't think for myself."

"We're neither of us young, dear," Mrs. Hartley said drily, "old people *are* a bit childish, you know."

Such flashes of realism in the even dullness of his wife's thought only irritated Mr. Hartley more.

"One thing is clear to me," he said sharply, "on this subject you'll never see sense. Celia gets worse and worse in her behaviour. Nurse Ramsay won't put up with it much longer and we'll never get another nurse nowadays."

Mrs. Hartley set out the patience cards on the little table. "Celia's always very sweet with me," she said, "I don't see what Nurse has to grumble at."

"My dear," Mr. Hartley said and his tone was tender and soothing, "be reasonable. It can't be very pleasant you know—all those rages and the difficulty with feeding, and really she's less able to be clean in her habits than two years ago."

The coarseness of the old man's allusion made Mrs. Hartley's hand tremble. She said nothing, however, but "red on black." Her silence encouraged her husband

"I want your help, Alice, over this, can't you see that? Don't force me to act alone. Come over with me and see this place at Dagmere, you're so much better at judging these things than I am."

Mrs Hartley was silent for a few minutes, then,

"Very well," she said, "we'll drive over to-morrow."
But her daughter's voice was in her ears. "I'm leaving
her with you, Mother, I know she'll be in good hands."

Celia was on the deck of the ship, the sun shone
brightly, the gongs beat, the whistles blew and her pink
hair ribbons were flying in the wind. All the stair rails
were painted bright red, pillar box red like blood, and
that was Celia's favourite colour. Red meant we must
stop, so Celia stopped. The gentleman in the postman's
suit came up to her. "Go on," he said, "don't stand
there gaping like a sawney." She wanted to tell him that
it was red and that she couldn't go, but the whistles and
the gongs made such a noise that he couldn't hear her.
"Go on," he cried, and he clapped his hands over her
head. Such a wind blew when he clapped his hands that
her hair ribbons blew off. Celia began to cry. "A nice
thing if every little girl cried when her ribbons blew
away," said Nurse Ramsay. She hoped to make Celia
run after them, although it was red and that meant we
must stop. But there was Granny beckoning to her and
there were the hair ribbons dancing in the sunshine a
little way ahead—they were two little pink dolls. So
Celia ran, although it was red. And now the side of the
ship had gone and great waves came up to pull her down,
green and grey. "Mummy, Mummy," she cried, but
the waves were folding over her. Mummy would not
come, and suddenly there was Mummy holding out her
arms to save her—Mummy all in blue. Celia ran into
her mother's arms and she sobbed on her mother's

bosom, she would not be lonely now, now she was safe. But Celia's Mummy's arms folded tight round her neck, tighter and tighter. "Don't, Mummy, don't. You're hurting me," Celia cried, and she looked up to see her mummy's eyes cruel and hard like Nurse Ramsay's. Celia began to scream and to fight, but her mummy's hands closed more and more tightly around her neck, crushing and pulping.

Nurse Ramsay heard the screams as she came up the dark drive. The battery in her torch had given out and she was feeling her way beside the wet bushes. The screams penetrated slowly into her consciousness, for she was oppressed by the memory of that humiliating scene at the Flannel Hop when Ivy had made such a fool of her in front of Ronnie Armitage. "Really it's getting impossible," she thought at first, "you can't leave her alone for half an hour now without trouble." Then suddenly something in the screams made her quicken her pace, and now she was running in panic, the branches of the rhododendron and laurel bushes catching at her like long spiky arms.

When she reached Celia's bedroom, it was already too late. No efforts of poor old Mr. Hartley or even of Goddard could bring life back to those flushed, purple cheeks, that swollen black neck. Dr. Lardner, who came shortly after, said that death was due as much to failure of the heart as to strangulation. "She must have woken herself in struggling to free her neck from the woollen jacket," he said, "and the fright acted upon an already weakened heart." It was easy to believe as one surveyed the body: the wreck of a great Britannia blonde, thirteen stone at least—she had put on weight ever since her twenty-fifth year—the round blue eyes might have fascinated had they not stared in childish idiocy, the masses of golden hair won praise had they not sprouted in tufts on the great pink cheeks, allying the poor lunatic to the animal world, marking her off from normal men and women.

Nurse Ramsay said the whole thing was a judgment. "If they hadn't been so obstinate and had agreed to send her to a proper home she'd have been alive to-day," she added. But Mrs. Hartley, who was a religious woman, offered thanks to God that night that Death had come in time to prevent her being taken away. "It's almost as though her mother had come to help her when she was in trouble," she thought.

Heart of Elm

"You work on the principle that grief brings hunger, Mother," said Thomas, as he sat on the edge of the kitchen table, swinging his legs and whistling "Eternal Father" under his breath.

"They're coming a long way" said Constance, spreading the fish paste more thickly than she would have done for persons of her own class. "Open that tin of tongue for me, darling." Last night's vigil had added dark brownish creases to her ravaged, over-painted face.

"That you should have sent for them is what beats me," said Katharine, who was pressing her nose and forehead against the cool window pane.

"Katharine," said Constance sharply, "do we have to?" She had not had time to do her hair properly, and its hennaed strands kept falling across her face, distracting her from the sandwiches, denying her the absorption that self-control demanded. "I've said that they're her family and you haven't thought that that mattered. . ."

Katharine turned towards her mother, her fresh complexioned face quite unmarked by the strain of events, her golden hair, her tweeds, her pearls as neat, as "nice young girl" as usual; only a hard glint in her blue eyes and the tension of her square jaw suggesting a certain hysteria. "A family who never come near her, who mean no more than strangers." She stood, legs apart, boyish, sincere, the only one who felt too much to voice her feelings.

"Jack?" asked Thomas, drawling. He found his sister's silent heroism more than he could bear. After all, capacity for self-expression is not incompatible with true feeling, he thought. It was a habit with him to clothe his thoughts in such phrases, as though the conciseness of their phraseology guaranteed the purity of the emotion. Almost immediately, however, to spite him, another voice inside him repeated the vulgar jingle that had been sounding in his head all the morning, "Part of my heart is dying upstairs," and tears welled up automatically into his eyes. He blushed as though the others might have heard; but, having convicted himself of self-pity and insincerity, he felt at once lighter, more free.

"Oh! the brother, perhaps," cried Katharine, and she frowned deeply for a moment, like a schoolboy with a "hard problem." "Yes, he and Ellen must have had fun in the early days . . ." she smiled at her own especial lien on the dying woman's memories. "But those *sisters*, I can't see . . ."

Constance laid down the bread knife. "Look," she said. "Upstairs Ellen is getting some relief and sleep with morphia, but for us it's quite different, this is our *worst* time. It may be an hour, Katharine, before you can boil another kettle or fill another hot water bottle, before you can start playing your part again," she put her hand on the girl's arm, and added softly, but reluctantly, for she felt no sympathy, only a desire to prevent an outburst, "before we can *all* start to play our parts again. *Now* we've got to face what we really feel. Do let us avoid scenes and bickering, if only to please Ellen," she noted that Thomas smiled contemptuously, but

Katharine's anger was appeased. "Don't let us be together too much. We all have our particular memories and sadnesses, and we'll be better on our own with them." She had touched the prefect in her daughter, who bent and kissed her, and even Thomas stopped whistling for a moment to give her a smile.

It's only for myself really, she thought, as she put on her goloshes to go out into the wet garden, *they* know what they feel, or rather they *think* they know and that's enough for them. Suddenly as she stepped out into the cold air and looked at the withered chrysanthemums, blackened by frost, her own feelings rushed through the barriers she had built up so carefully in the devitalized air of her early morning watch by the bedside. I feel nothing but relief, she thought, it's the first step towards my freedom from all this, and with her heel she dug the last faded yellow flower head into the ground. It won't be long now before I've done with all these boring gentlewomen's tasks, this freezing my hands with damp and mud to avoid the suffocating cosiness of their family life indoors. She had realized something of this relief the night before as the old woman's brown eyes had followed her every movement with dogged devotion. Against that loyalty and that dependence she had been unable to fight, as they had twined her and the children into a family knot that had grown ever tighter in the past ten years; against that background of loyalty and dependence Thomas and Katharine had failed to grow up, had clung to well-thumbed books and fretsaw sets, had bolstered their incompetence with Ellen's uncomprehending admiration; and she, who had woken to her scorn of it too late to act without hurting, had sought refuge from the dumb gaze in the garden that she hated. But now she would go to London, and read and do things for themselves, not for their associations or memories. She began to sing a favourite song of her uncle's, as she tore the chrysanthemum plants from the wet soil—"*Let's all go down the Strand, have a banana.*"

The faintest sound from Ellen's room caught Katharine's keyed-up attention, and she was soon bending low over the old woman, whose bulk seemed to have shrunk to nothing in the huge fourposter, but whose flushed features stood out like the full moon of a child's drawing against the heaped white pillows. It was only a momentary return from the drugged sleep that had roused her, and Katharine could hardly catch the whispered, twisted words that came from the fallen mouth. Her pride demanded an interpretation, however, and she began to deal with the bedpan as the nurse had shown her, when she realized that something further was amiss. "Get him out, get that one out" the old woman was saying. Looking up, she saw Thomas standing silently by the foot of the bed, his hearing only a shade less acute than her own. "Not now, Thomas," she whispered, "she doesn't want you here at such a time. It's upsetting her," and to the old woman, "he's just going, darling. He didn't realize he was in the way, the old silly," and she smiled as she saw the worried features relax.

Thomas walked along the corridor, running his hand against the doorposts, and whistling "Eternal Father" slightly more loudly than he himself could bear. He smiled to think that poor old Ellen's prudery should cast him as a stranger at such times. It was not, he almost said to himself, as if he was a man, he was Master Thomas. Why it was Ellen who had wept so bitterly when he had been called up for National Service—"You can say what you like, Madam," she had said, "but that Government won't do us no good that mixes gentlemen like Mr. Thomas with all that rifferty rafferty," Katharine and he had always used "rifferty rafferty" in their private language to which Ellen had unconsciously contributed so much, so that the sentiment had been particularly pleasing to him. As he passed each door, he remembered consciously how he had "mooched" like this in the past, always to an invisible audience crying, "Hard luck, old man," or "Don't you believe it, things will come out in the end just as you want them." Of course, they hadn't, but he was still in the same house with the same comforting voices. Smiling a little cynically in self-deprecation, he went into his work room and began planing the wood for the new bookcase to replace the last he had made, which had fallen to pieces so much sooner than was to be expected.

A quarter of an hour later, Constance came indoors and threw aside the gardening gloves she detested. She smiled contentedly as she went upstairs to indulge in her favourite, enervating orgy of an overperfumed hot bath before the relatives began to arrive. "All amongst the girls and bhoys"—it had to be bhoys she remembered—"kicking up a fearful noise" she sang softly, the words were probably incorrect, but the picture was an attractive one. Passing the nursery door she saw Katharine lying on her stomach on the hearthrug, reading some favourite book—*Little Women*, no doubt, or an E. Nesbitt—from the workroom she could hear Thomas's hymn tune above the noise of the plane. She felt her whole body tremble with anger, with self-reproach, with shame. She tried hard to tell herself that she must say nothing in rage, but another voice reasoned that without this fury she would never speak, that she would be beaten into submission. In ten years' time she would be Ellen's age, would need the children physically as Ellen needed them; before the horror of that, all restraint vanished. "Thomas," she called, "would you come into the nursery for a moment?"

With her back to the window, her bad make-up and spraying dyed hair looked peculiarly garish. It took all Katharine's energy to resist embarrassment when she was forced to see her mother clearly like this.

"If Ellen dies, and we must remember that Dr. Martley says he can do nothing." Constance tried to make her voice as kind as she could, "I shall give up this house, my dears, and go to live in London."

Katharine made a determined effort at self-deception. "Don't worry, Mummy," she said, "even if everything should go wrong, I'm sure we could manage. I know it seems impossible to imagine life without her, but I'll do everything I can to help you to carry on somehow."

"That's very kind of you, Katharine, but I don't wish to carry on. I want to go away to London, and live by myself. I couldn't do anything whilst Ellen was with us, especially in these last years when her health's been so bad, but if she dies, I can and I shall."

"And us?" said Thomas. He disliked sharing Katharine's hostility to their mother, but it was impossible to forget that Father had left them as a sacred trust to her, Ellen had often told them so. "You seem to forget that I took this filthy job at Acrewood to be near you."

"No, Thomas, you took it in order to live at home. To be in comfort and not to have to grow up. When you came out of the army, I advised you against it; but you hadn't finished making the new hen-house, so of course, you couldn't take a job away from home."

"And what about Katharine?" said Thomas. "Do you think she wants to be cooped up in the country here, where she never meets any men from one month to another?"

"Thomas, please," Katharine almost broke her necklace, as she clutched at the pearls in protest. "I stay here because it's my home. I was brought up here, I love it, and I don't intend to leave it."

"No, Katharine, nor does Thomas," said Constance, "not while there are old drawers of photos to turn out, or dressing-up boxes to laugh over; not while you can still cut out clothes badly for Ellen to smile over and alter behind your back. But perhaps you won't feel quite the same when Ellen is gone."

"How can you speak like that, Mother?" cried Katharine. "After *all* she did for you when Daddy died. Or perhaps you'll say that she lied."

"No, darling, Ellen was speaking the truth. I was quite hopeless in the house. You see I hadn't been brought up as a gentlewoman, only as a rich man's daughter. *Nouveau riche* your father's sisters called me, it meant that I couldn't make pickles for toffee, or toffee for pickles for that matter," Constance seldom made a joke, so that she felt rather pleased, "but I *was* brought up to believe in drive."

"Oh! guts," said Thomas.

"Yes, as vulgar as that," his mother replied. Thomas knew that shame would soon capture him, and to fight his natural drift towards surrender he concentrated on his mother's share of the blame for not forcing the issue earlier. Katharine remembered only Ellen's devotion and the happiness of their home; she repeated to herself tragically. "My mother is a wicked woman."

Even Katharine, however, felt relieved when the noise of a motor-bike on the gravel drive prevented any further dramatic development. "So much for myself," said Constance, "from now on, whilst Ellen lives, her needs must override everything else." It would seem, thought Thomas, as he watched his mother's gesture with her jewelled hand, that exploitation of dramatic possibilities is not confined to the cowardly dreamers of this world. The phrase restored much of his self-esteem. Nevertheless he hung back behind the women as they ushered in their visitor. So this was Jack, Ellen's black sheep brother, a little elderly man with spectacles and a grizzled moustache who looked like Kipling, dressed incongruously in a full suit of daffodil yellow waterproof.

"So very little I'm afraid can be done, Mr. Gilmore," Constance was saying. "Nurse comes in to administer the morphia. Sleep may do some good, you see, and . . ."

The little man looked impressed, "Ah! morphia that'd be it," he said, shaking his head, "no doubt they'd find a use for that."

It was curious that he should be so ignorant, thought Thomas, when one remembered Ellen's delight in telling them how her brother "had wedded and buried three lawful, and as many that he never took to church."

It was when he was taking off his waterproofs, that Mr. Gilmore turned to Katharine, his wrinkled, coppery, ex-sailor's face blurred in a smile. "It wouldn't do at all to be wearing them yallerey things in the sick room," he said, "proper scandalizing that'd be," and he winked. He'll use that charm to get Ellen's property if there's time, thought Thomas, in one of his sudden flashes of observation.

Ellen was struggling to sit up when they entered her room. Sleep had reduced the flushed, swollen look of her features, and now that coherence was replacing the drug-shattered speech she seemed almost convalescent.

"Well, gel," was Mr. Gilmore's greeting, "what are you getting me over here like this for? You're more like ready to take on a second than leaving us yet awhile."

Ellen's body was convulsed with chuckles so that Thomas was quite alarmed. It was clear that any reference to marriage by Mr. Gilmore was irresistibly funny to his sister. "Ow, Lor, Jack Gilmore," she said, "it's clear *you* haven't changed."

"Not for better nor for worse," said Mr. Gilmore, to his sister's delight.

"So you've met Mr. Thomas," said Ellen. "Didn't I tell you what a fine gentleman 'e'd grown up to be?"

Mr. Gilmore grunted, he was clearly not very impressed with Thomas.

"What do you think?" said Ellen outraged. "Tried to make him a soldier. I don't understand it. Why! it used to be no one went for a soldier unless he had something to be ashamed on. Making gentlemen into soldiers!" she snorted.

"There's worse than soldiers, come to that," said her brother.

"Yes," the old woman brought out with a violent effort to suppress her own laughter, "there's sailors."

The old man slapped his thigh. "You'm old devil," he laughed, in excitement his grammar was completely at sea.

" 'Ow do you like our Miss Katharine?" asked Ellen, "Isn't she pretty?" "I should shay sho," laughed her brother. He had a stock of such phrases from troop entertainments of World War I of which he was very proud. " 'E always liked a pretty face," said Ellen "and other pretty things too." It was not the Ellen that Thomas and Katharine knew. They, however, were soon forgotten in the rapid interchange of reminiscence and gossip between the two old people, a conversation which seemed to take Ellen further and further from their recognition.

"So Bill Darrett goes and gets married does 'e?" Ellen was saying. "The owd fool."

"Owd fool's not 'alf of it," laughed Jack. "She worn't turned twenty and 'im sixty-foive. 'This is going to be alright, Jack,' 'e says to me. It wor. 'E burst a bloody blood vessel first noite, the silly bugger." Behind the riotous laughter, Tom was visibly shocked. Katharine noted this in time and assumed an expression of human understanding that established her more complete identification with Ellen most satisfactorily.

She would have been happier with her own family all the time, thought Constance, as she came into the room. The irony seemed complete.

"You'd like something to eat and drink I'm sure, Mr. Gilmore," she said, "after your long journey."

"Don't you go giving a lot of trouble now," called Ellen, but she was clearly hard put to it to distinguish between the claims of two such different yet long established duties.

"She'll be alright, I think, don't you, Mr. Gilmore?" asked Katharine cheerfully, as they walked downstairs.

"No," the old man replied, "she won't last the night. She's 'ad 'er day alright, but they all take it 'ard in going . . . Get a bit funny they do sometimes, but Ellen's alright, she's not the sort to forget 'er family," and he gave his hosts a look designed to destroy any material hopes that they might cherish.

Constance's belief in Ellen's family attachment was not to be sustained, however, on the arrival of the youngest sister, Kitty. Mrs. Temple emerged from her car, shy and defiant, determined to establish social equality before she could be patronized. Her son Len had left his café for the day to drive her over, and the journey had assumed an atmosphere of festivity which they found it hard to throw off before the obligations of convention. Beneath a profusion of fox fur and eye veil something of Ellen could be seen in Kitty—a tendency to wink irrelevantly and a swollen look of suppressed raucous laughter that suggested a fun fair. She and her son were resolute in their adherence to small talk as they mounted the stairs.

"Very hard on owner drivers." "So funny to see the roads so deserted." "Terrible to see all the old houses up for sale." "Quite happy as long as they've got the picture houses to go to." Mrs. Temple's genteely distorted voice managed to fill a remarkably short space of time with a considerable commentary. Eyeing Constance's make-up she had grave doubts of Ellen's beloved "family," but Katharine's pearls and tweeds set her fears at rest.

There were no doubts, however, about Ellen's feelings towards her smart sister, she opened one eye, closed it resolutely and withdrew herself into sleep. She allowed her nephew to take her hand, as he said brightly. "Well, Auntie Ellen, what's all this about? Never mind, you'll be alright now, we're all here to keep you company," but she immediately withdrew it, and, turning her head away, mumbled that she was tired. "She were as bright as a bee till you come, Kitty" said Jack. Mrs. Temple affected not to hear. It was really very difficult, she thought, Ellen ought never to have stayed in service, she had plenty of money saved up, but there it was, she was always obstinate, and now they were stuck in this house, and Gracious knew what to do.

"I think we'd better leave her for a bit," said Constance,

"Take Mrs. Temple to the drawing room, Thomas."

"Well, I'm sure I don't know," said Kitty embarrassedly. "You mustn't let us be a trouble, Mrs. Graham.
I know what the morning's like." Then she paused,
blushing for fear that she had made some unsuitable
allusion to the domestic situation in the house. "We'll
just go for a little drive and perhaps when we get back
she'll be ready to see us." But Thomas was not going to
forgo his duty. He had been asked to suffer this im-
position, when his heart was full, and he would do so.
He was not entirely unconscious, also, of the pleasure
which he would derive from putting himself over these
people, their simple response to his grief would perhaps
still his gnawing doubts of his own sincerity. To suppose
that her family would be easily moved on the subject of
Ellen was a slight miscalculation; to them her courage
and resolution seemed merely obstinacy, her idiosyn-
cratic speech and behaviour a social embarrassment, her
strangely vivid narratives a tedious bore; nevertheless
Thomas's powers of persuasion were great, in particular
where he felt quite sincerely the emotions which he was
consciously arranging for his audience, and in a short
while his three listeners were deeply moved. It was
"Ladies and gentlemen! I give you Ellen!" and Ellen
he gave them with a vengeance, in particular, Ellen as
he had known her, as she had responded to him, as no
one but he could quite have understood her. It was
"I remember once when we were quite kids, Mrs.
Temple . . .," or "Whether it was I had a special way
with her or not I don't know, but . . .," or again, "It
was a long time before she would tell even me, and even

then it was typical of her courage and her thought for others that I was sworn to secrecy. . . ." He gave them humorous stories of her, too, carefully arranged so as not to make too much of her rusticity which might embarrass them—"If you had seen our uncle Alfred, Mr. Gilmore, you'd know just how good 'old poll parrot impertinence' was to describe him." Once or twice he felt himself going beyond the comprehension of his audience, and it was then that he hit upon the phrase that took their fancy so completely—"She is, you know," he said "a real heart of oak," and Mr. Gilmore, who himself had something of a histrionic streak, said with a throb in his voice, "That's it, that's our Ellen, a real heart of oak." After that it was repeated by the family a hundred times, it gave them just the cue they needed. Kitty was so moved that her little eye-veil shook and bobbed, and her voice lost much of its frightened gentility as she took Thomas's hand. "She had a true friend in you alright. Dear old Ellen! the times we used to have . . ." and her eyes were clouded with tears. But Thomas's final triumph came from Len. With more sophistication and education, Len was somewhat mistrustful of a man of his own age with so much to say. Stiff and uneasy, he stood with serious, doubtful gaze whilst the others responded— in his good grey flannels and smart sports-coat a great contrast to his Uncle Jack in shiny best blue serge. At last, however, he, too, was moved and, crossing the room, he solemnly shook Thomas's hand, "Thanks, old man," he said, "for all you've done for the old lady." It was Thomas's greatest victory—he had sanctified

Ellen, he had vindicated himself, and now for a while he would be tranquil, until his self-loathing should recount the whole episode again to him in mocking, painful terms.

It was lucky for Thomas that the last member of Ellen's family—Lottie, the eldest, unmarried sister who had brought them all up—was not present at his recital, for she was unlikely to have responded. She had, in fact, entered the house unnoticed, largely because of the general absorption in Thomas's elegy. Constance was the first to see this little, dried up old woman in black. She suddenly appeared in the bathroom whilst Constance was gargling—it was typical of Constance that the strain of the day should suddenly have impelled her to gargle. She thought at first that this must be someone sent by the nurse, but the little old woman said "Miss Gilmore, Madam, Lottie, Ellen's sister," and from the mixture of respect and reserve Constance knew that, from that time on, Lottie would be in charge. It's she who should have been called Ellen, and Ellen Lottie, she thought. "I should like to see my sister at once, if you please, madam" said Lottie, and followed this by a series of questions concerning the nature of her sister's illness, the views of the doctor, and the duties performed by the nurse. Over the latter she clicked her tongue in disapproval several times, but at the end she only said "Well I'm sure it's a blessing, madam, you were all here when it happened. There'll be no occasion to bother you any further, it's for her family to take on now." Constance

dreaded, but with a certain relish, the impact of Lottie
upon Katharine.

Sure enough, when they entered the sick room
Katharine stood by the side of the bed, holding a hot
water bottle as though she were presenting arms. "My
daughter" said Constance. "Good evening, Miss," said
Lottie, then going up to Ellen, who seemed restless and
flushed, she said "There, there, there's no need to take
on or fret, it's me—Lottie." She rearranged the pillows
with clicks of disapproval. For a moment Ellen seemed
to recognize her, and smiled like a satisfied child. "Ah!"
said Lottie, "The poor soul's glad to see her own folk.
Shop clothes will wear very well, but there's nothing
like home-mades when all's said and done." Soon
Ellen began to fidget and mumble again. "Ow we *was*
poor," she seemed to be saying, and Lottie said gently,
"So we was, dearie, as poor as poor, but there's no need
to take on with it now." Yet when Katharine asked her
eagerly if she understood what the sick woman seemed
so anxious to tell, the little old woman only replied
"Just ramblings and talk, Miss. She won't last long
now, She's struggling against what must be. It's lucky
she's not more rumbustious." Then more authoritatively
she added, "Would you please to send my nephew for
the nurse, and tell my sister she's wanted up here,"
and taking the hot water bottle from Katharine, she
said "I'll see to that, Miss."

After their notice to quit, Constance, Katharine and
Thomas sat in the hall, waiting for news. Nurse informed
them that the end was near, and once Jack appeared at
the top of the stairs to ask for some brandy, though it

was not quite clear for whom. It seemed as though the Grahams had played their part and would be needed no more, when suddenly Lottie herself appeared on the landing above them, "Would you come, Madam?" she asked Constance, "She's asking for you badly."

When Constance entered the bedroom, Ellen was struggling to be free of the nurse's hold, her face flushed, her eyes streaming with tears, but on Constance's approach, she grasped her arms as though with talons and drew her towards her. "My dearie, my lovie" she mumbled. Stiff and rigid, Constance held the old woman in her arms as she died.

Lottie took charge once more after her sister's death, assisting the nurse in the laying-out, clicking in disapproval at the inadequacy of the napkins provided, sending Len to fetch the undertaker, watching with a jealous eye over Kitty and Jack as they made a preliminary survey of Ellen's "things." Once again Constance and her children sat in isolation in the hall. Thomas and Katharine were too submerged in memories, felt too wild a desire to force the past to return, for any conscious expression of their grief, but Constance sat frozen with horror. Nothing can be worse than that, she thought. As through the last days she had become conscious of the indifference, even the hostility towards Ellen which she had suppressed all these years, she had comforted herself with the thought that it must surely be reciprocated. They had, after all, been no more than two women forced by circumstances to work together for so long; and, Ellen, with her worship of the children, must have guessed and resented her own criticism of them. But now this prop on which she had supported her determination to escape had been beaten out of her hand; it was clearly she whom Ellen had adored, she could not deceive herself about that, however stiffly she had held the dying woman, she knew that she was holding the person who had loved her more than anyone ever would, and that calculatedly she must betray that love. Characteristically she had put on fresh make-up after the death, but her skin showed drawn and pale around the rouge, as she sat puffing nervily at a cigarette and holding on to her resolve. "I said 'Whilst Ellen lives,'" she kept repeating, "not after."

Some time later Len returned with the undertaker, a little, suave man with ill-fitting false teeth. Kitty came downstairs to meet them, her fox fur and eye-veil resumed for the occasion. "And what age was the lady?" asked the undertaker humbly. Any question of age made Kitty coy, and she traced patterns on the carpet with her toe, as she replied, "Oh, well, about ten years older than me. Yes, that's right, Ellen was ten years older than me."

"Ah!" said the undertaker, all diplomacy, as they passed upstairs, "a middle-aged lady, then elm wood would be preferred."

Constance began to laugh. Both the children in whose eyes she had acquired a new status by her summons at the end—like Moses to Sinai—took her hands, "Hush, darling," they said proud of their recognition of hysteria. But Constance shook their hands away,

"I was only just thinking—not heart of *oak*, you know, at all, heart of *elm*." Something in her voice made Katharine stiffen. This is their battle at last, thought Thomas as his sister spoke, I shall withdraw.

"Well?" said Katharine coldly. "She *was* like an elm tree, you know. A great elm under which we all sheltered, to which all of us clung." "Oh! yes," replied Constance, "she was like an elm tree. But understand this, there aren't any more elm trees, no more hearts of elm."

What do Hippo's Eat?

SHE seemed such a little bit of a thing as she peered through the railings at the huge, cumbrous bison, her neat boyish head of short-cut, tight red curls such a contrast to the matted chocolate wool that lay in patches around the beast's long, mournful features. "Ginger for pluck" Maurice always called her, and indeed her well-knit little figure and firm stance were redolent of determination and cheek, and cried out her virtues as a real good pal, her Dead End Kid appeal that went through to the heart.

"My! My!" she said to the bison, "someone forgot to bring his comb." She was such a round-eyed urchin that one felt almost surprised when she did not put out her tongue.

Maurice smiled paternally and fingered his little grey first world war moustache. "How would you like to have a couple of rounds in the ring with that?" he asked laughing.

"Oh! I'd take it on all right," she said, and gave him one of her funny straight looks. She had only two roles with men—tomboy and good scout—even they were very alike, except that the good scout was full of deep, silent understanding and could hold her drink.

Maurice guffawed, "My God! I believe you would. Size means nothing to you." His admiration was perfectly genuine, for under his ostentatious virility he was a physically timorous man with a taste for the brutal. As he looked appraisingly at her slender shoulders and tight little breasts, he felt wonderfully protective and sentimental. All the same it irked him that he wasn't getting on faster with his scheme. It was true, he reflected, that he hadn't paid a sausage out in rent for the last two months and she'd cashed two stumers for him without batting an eyelid when they came back "R.D."; but now that he'd turned fifty-five he wanted a more secure berth than that. The truth was that Maurice had experienced some unpleasant bouts of giddiness in the mornings recently, and his heart—he called it "the old ticker" even to himself—often missed a beat when he climbed upstairs. Under such circumstances, a partnership in the boarding house—it was his name for legalized use of her capital--would just suit him, with a liberal supply of pocket money for the "dogs." Earls Court wasn't exactly the neighbourhood he would have chosen, indeed, when he remembered his brief residence in Clarges Street, now seen in retrospect as lasting for years, he felt ashamed that he should have sunk so low, but he had known too much of Camden Town and the York Road, Waterloo, in the interval not to count his blessings while they lasted. He was, in fact, worn out with schemes and lies and phoney deals, he slept badly and his nerves were giving way. Temporary setbacks made him act, as now, precipitately.

"It's grand to see you enjoying yourself, Greta," he said. "You ought to be having lots of fun whilst you're still young. It's a damned shame the way you have to work. You had a hard enough life as a kid, God knows, and now this blasted house hanging round your neck.

It's too much even for your heavyweight shoulders," and he laughed.

Greta stuck out her chin, "I had my fun all right," she said. "You don't have to be rich to enjoy life as a kid."

"Oh, I know," Maurice replied, with a smile as though she had been referring to hopscotch in the back alley. "You can take it on the chin all right, I'll say that for you. But all the same," he continued with a sigh, "I'd give my right hand to have known you when I still had a bit of money. *I'd* have put an end to all these worries."

Greta had decided not to notice Maurice's remarks for a few moments, so she turned to watch a scarlet ibis wading in the pool behind them.

"Aren't you a lucky bird not to be a hat?" she asked. She had her special brand of humour—the gang at the local called it "Greta's dopey jokes." Then, "You're my only money worry, Maurice Legge," she said, her Manchester accent more emphasized than usual, "and what are you going to do about *that*?"

Self-pity and suppressed anger brought beads of sweat to his temples and he mopped them with the silk handkerchief which he kept in his cuff—an old ex-officer habit, he was always careful to explain. Two pictures flashed before him in quick succession. First, the young ex-subaltern, a possible for the Harlequins; handsome, easy-going; a man to whom stockbrokers offered £2,000 a year jobs on his social contacts alone. Then the other picture—still a handsome man, old and tired now, but unmistakably a gentleman for all the doubtful shifts into which life had forced him—he bent before the cheap snubs and insults of a common little creature, whom the ex-subaltern would not have noticed in, a crowd. He could almost hear the commentator say, "Look upon this picture and on *this*," and his eyes filled with tears. This cinematographic representation of life had grown on him in middle age. It was not a surprising phenomenon, since his days were passed in a highly coloured histrionic blur. He would move from Prince's to the Cri, from the Cri to the Troc, from the Troc to Odennino's, trying with a closely-knit web of circumstantial narrative to pull off complicated deals or, at the very least, to cadge a drink from some toughly sentimental whisky-soaking Colonial or American. In the intervals of this "work," he went to the "pictures" or sat before the gasfire of his bed-sitting room working out large betting schemes which he had not the capital to realize, or reading cheap thrillers. Past, present and future, truth and lies, all moved before him in short, vivid, dramatic scenes that merged into a background mist of anxiety, imagined grandeur and sticky sentiment. But behind it all was a certain hard core of determination to survive. It was this that made him swallow Greta's snub and turn to the buffaloes.

"Nice mild-looking fellows, you would say about those, wouldn't you?" he asked. Greta looked at their large, brown calf's eyes and their shapely horns, and nodded.

"How wrong you'd be," said Maurice. "I shall never forget once up country from Nairobi going through a village after buffalo had stampeded. Not a pleasant sight at all. Harry Brand was with me and I've never seen a chap turn so green. 'So help me, God, Maurice,' he said, 'I shall have to call it a day and turn back.' Funny thing, really, because he was a beefy sort of cove. But you remember him, anyhow."

Greta shook her head. "Oh yes you do, darling," said Maurice, "great red-faced fellow we met one evening outside the Plaza." Greta looked puzzled but denied it. "I'm sure you did," Maurice went on. Then he added thoughtfully, "But wait a minute though, perhaps you're right. Yes, you are. I was with Dolly." And, glad to have checked this point, he returned to Kenya with renewed ardour.

Greta listened to his stories with rapt attention. However her business acumen and natural hardness might protect her against his wilder financial schemes, her pride and delight in his recounted exploits were for once in her life quite unselfconsciously childlike. His attraction as a gentleman was enhanced for her by the cosmopolitan background which every day of their intimacy revealed a little more. She felt, more justly than she realized, that it was an authentication of all that the films had hinted to her. The digressions, irrelevant ramifications and long-winded checks of memory in which Maurice indulged might have been expected to bore his listeners, but strangely enough they were exactly the features which finally convinced the sceptical, banishing suspicions of glibness and lending realism to art. To Greta they were the supreme pleasure, for they seemed somehow to involve her own participation in these exciting adventures. After all she had, it seemed, only just missed meeting Harry Brand outside the Plaza. For Maurice himself they formed a reassurance which his self-confidence badly needed. He had told so many stories for so many years, truth and fiction were so inextricably mixed, that to check a new falsehood by a poorly remembered old one made him feel that in some way truth must be involved somewhere.

As they walked into the Lion House Maurice felt his confidence returning. He was ready for any audience. And there, gazing at the Siberian tiger, an audience awaited him—an elderly solicitor and his wife, a working-class woman with two small children. Maurice began to talk to Greta in a voice pitched loudly enough for the others to hear.

"Siberian tiger, eh?" he said. "A present from our not such dear friends the Russians. He's a beautiful creature, though. Never had any experience with them myself, but I should think they might be very ugly customers. Don't you agree, sir?" he asked the solicitor, who replied embarrassedly, "Yes, yes, I should imagine so."

"No," said Maurice loudly and self-deprecatingly. "I've only run across this chap's Indian cousin who's altogether smaller fry. Most of this stuff about man-eaters, you know, is a lot of nonsense. No tiger turns to human flesh until he's too old to hold his own in the jungle."

"Do you hear that, Billy?" said the woman to her son.

"Oh, yes," Maurice continued, "all these round-ups of tigers for important people, makes you laugh if you know about it, half the poor blighters can hardly stand up with old age. So if anyone asks you to a tiger shoot, laddy," he said to the boy, "you can be sure of bringing your mother back a nice new rug."

"There you are, Billy," said the woman, "you hear what the gentleman says," and everyone laughed.

Greta felt so proud of Maurice. He looked so handsome, despite all his wrinkles and pouches, and the line of his arm appeared so strong and manly as he gripped the rail in front of him, that she longed to take his hand in hers and to stroke it. He had told her so often, however, that physical caresses in public were "just not done," and she was able now to check herself in time. Greta was both anxious and quick to learn as she climbed up the economic ladder, and she felt it was one of the great advantages of her relations with Maurice that he could teach her so much. She no longer said "serviette" or dropped her shoes off under restaurant tables. She never went out now without gloves—Maurice's ideas of polite behaviour belonged rather to his early years—but she also no longer blew into them when she took them off. She could hardly guess that he had mixed little with respectable people of any class for over fifteen years, and thus she was able to retain many of her humorous phrases— "he's a smell on the landing to me" was a favourite— without qualms, for Maurice greeted them with a smile. She was jealous sometimes of his larking with waitresses, but he told her not to be suburban, and in any case she felt ready to forgive anything as she watched him finger the knot of his old school tie whilst he studied the menu, and heard him refer to her as "Madam" when he finally gave the order.

As the keeper passed the tiger cage with a bucket of dung Maurice asked him which the biggest lion was now

and how many pounds of meat the black leopard con-
sumed in a day. He was one of the older keepers and
received Maurice's officer-to-batman manner in a more
friendly spirit than was often the case these days. Soon
the whole party was being taken behind the scenes to
watch a puma cross one of the little bridges to its outdoor
cage. Greta felt quite queenly when she saw the respectful
manner in which the keeper received Maurice's tip, and
she attempted a new charming bow and smile as the
party broke up.   She even approved Maurice's giving
sixpence to the two little children, though in general she
did not care to spend her money too lavishly.

Maurice looked ten years younger as they walked away
from the Lion House. He had always been interested in
wild animals, felt a mastery over them that he lacked
with men, and these boyish sensations combined with a
genuine aesthetic feeling for their shape and colour were
now re-awakened. It was so seldom that he experienced
any pleasure divorced from his own schemes and anxieties
these days, and his body expanded and revelled in the
carefree mood. He stroked the soft nose of the caribou
as it pushed through the bars in quest of food. It was not,
therefore, surprising that he felt little pleasure in Greta's
urchin impudence when she gave the animal the raspberry. But he was too happy to comment on her vulgarity.
For her, wild animals were an alarming and remote tribe,
that once secured behind bars or in travelling circuses,
could be treated as comic turns.

But Greta's thoughts were not, in any case, on the
beasts, they were very much upon Maurice. She had
seldom felt him so desirable, and it worried her to see the

creases of his suit—so overcleaned and repaired—shine in the sunlight. She knew the pitiable state of his few underclothes and threadbare second suit as they reposed in the chest of drawers in a litter of important-looking papers, solicitors' letters, unpaid bills and pawntickets— knew only too well, for in the first weeks of his failure to pay his rent she had searched in vain for any saleable articles. Though she could not allow him to handle her money since he was obviously so foolish about business, he *was* her man and she wanted him to look nice. She made up her mind to buy him a whole new outfit. She had done very well out of letting her rooms in the last few years and could afford to spend a little and still leave the good margin in the bank which represented respectability to her. Greta's realism had begun at sixteen as a waitress, Maurice's had never really got going: it was hardly an even match. In her greater sense of reality she was far clearer about what she did and did not want. She wanted a man, and the fact that he was twenty years older did not trouble her, for she liked experience. Nevertheless she did not want to tie herself to someone who might play fast and loose with her savings, nor even perhaps would she want that man at all when he had passed sixty. However if he was not to have her money he should certainly have a suit.

Greta's friendly thoughts, her increased desire for him, communicated themselves to Maurice and, added to his own happy mood, made him walk on air. Tips passed lavishly as they fed the sealions from the rocks—Greta screamed and jumped like a little girl as the shapely, blubbery creatures flopped about her—gave honey to the brown bear—Maurice smiled in his old way as she cried "Who's got a bear behind?"—how devil-may-care he was with a carefully selected snake coiled round his arm! The monkeys rather damped their ardour, for they were both united in their prudish disapproval of certain antics. But an incident in front of the spider monkeys' cage finally broke up their happy mood. They were laughing delightedly as the monkeys snatched the bread they offered and swung away with feet, hands and tails alike, when a young couple approached the cage. In general Greta did not care for freaks and there was certainly something a bit cranky about the young woman's long, shapeless grey frock and the young man's corduroys and knapsack. They were, in fact, R.A.D.A. students at play. But their studied seriousness and carefully beautiful voices impressed Greta.

"Their movements *are* rather heavenly," said the girl. "Almost a ghostlike flitting."

"It's immensely interesting that they should have developed prehensile tails," said the boy, and seeing Greta watching him, he smiled the new shy smile he was developing to play Oswald in "Ghosts." Greta was completely conquered and smiled back. Maurice began to talk loudly, but Greta frowned impatiently, for the boy was speaking again.

"You see they're really gibbons, at least I think so," and he smiled shyly again, "and yet they've developed prehensile tails as well as arms and legs for swinging. It's a complete vindication of Lamarck really."

"You do find the oddest things interesting, darling," said the girl. Greta felt so angry with her.

"You can always learn something if you keep your ears open," she said and smiled again at the boy.

"Come along," said Maurice impatiently. "We don't want to watch these damned monkeys all day," but Greta waited a few minutes before following.

They stood surveying the hideous flat features of the lion-faced baboon in angry silence. "Why the hell you want to encourage that damned unwashed long-haired young swine," said Maurice, "I can't imagine."

"Because," replied Greta—she snapped like a turtle when she was annoyed—"I'm willing to learn from others occasionally."

"And you've got a hell of a lot to learn."

"I fully appreciate the lessons," Greta cried, "and I hope you appreciate what I pay for them."

Maurice's eyes narrowed with rage. "What exactly do you mean by that?"

"Two months' rent. That's what I mean by that, Maurice Legge." He raised his fist as though to hit her, and she ran from him, calling, "You keep away from me." An elderly woman turned to stare at them.

"I'll leave your bloody house to-night," he shouted. "You'll get your cheque to-morrow morning."

"Yes," said Greta, "and it'll come back R.D. by the end of the week."

"You little so-and-so," Maurice cried; it was one of his favourite phrases. He was trembling with rage, but behind his anger he could see all his hopes crumbling. He felt completely at the end of his tether; a night on the streets at his age might finish him off. With a tremendous effort he controlled his temper.

"Don't let's be greater fools than God made us," he said.

Greta watched his collapse with genuine pity, she felt more than ever determined to look after him. But first, like all men, he must be taught a lesson, a lesson for spoilt children. From the pages of her favourite woman's journal she recalled the advice, "He will accept you at the price you put on yourself, so don't make yourself cheap" —it was not exactly the situation the editress had in mind, but it seemed to apply.

"No thank you, Maurice. I've had enough. We're friends if you like, but friends apart," she felt very pleased with the phrase. Sturdy, jaunty, independent, she walked away from him, past the pelicans and the ravens, towards the tunnel. Maurice stood sullenly for a few minutes, then he ran after her. He saw her at the far end of the tunnel and shouted "Greta! Greta!" until his ears were filled with the echoes. His heart was pounding heavily and his legs felt like lead. He noticed the flood level mark and wished he were under the waters. Greta stood and waited for him.

"I'm sorry, kiddie," he said, "I can't say more."

"That's all right," she replied, the perfect good scout. "We'll say no more about it."

They went slowly back through the tunnel to the tearoom.

The "set" tea with watercress *ad lib* was like a children's picnic, as they laughed and teased away the memory of the angry outburst. Greta was determined to bring back Maurice's pleasure. She felt sure of her mastery now and was anxious to erase all trace of the events that had revealed it. She stuffed herself almost sick with bread and butter and buns, because he so delighted to tease her about her "kid's appetite." "Greedy guts," he said smiling, as she took a second helping of watercress. He was quite sentimental now, as he thought of where he would be without her generosity; she might not be a lady but she certainly had a heart of gold. Ever sanguine and tenacious, he began to consider new ways of putting his little scheme to her.

"Shall we have a dekko at the elephants and then make for home?" he asked.

As they passed through the tunnel once more, Greta thought how alike all men are, just children really, and she purred as she thought how well she understood him. When they approached the pool where the orange-teethed coypus sat on the rocks, cleaning their whiskers, she began to sing, "He's my guy. Heaven knows why I love him, but he's my guy."

"There's your famous musquash coats," said Maurice, pointing at the huge rats, with their wet, coarse bristles.

"I *should* believe you," Greta cried. They were both delighted when he convinced her—he because she was such a funny ignorant little rascal, she because it really was surprising what he knew. "Well I'll never have a musquash coat," she cried, "not from creatures with teeth like that."

They watched the otter as it swam in crazy circles round its pool, trying ceaselessly to dig a way through the concrete sides down to the open sea. "The way it keeps scrabbling," said Greta, "I should think it wanted to get out." They both had to laugh at its antics.

When they reached the Elephant House Maurice asked the keeper if they could go to the back of the hippopotamus pool. He was quite a young Cockney who didn't respond to Maurice's manner at all. "It's not usual," he said. "There's nothing to see, you know, that you can't see from here."

"All the same," replied Maurice, "I'd like to take the lady round the back."

"O.K. Colonel," the boy said, winking across at Greta, "but it's not the place I'd choose to take my girl friend."

It was, indeed, most unattractive on closer inspection. The hot steam from the muddy water smelt abominably and the sides of the pool were slippery with slime. Every now and again the huge black forms would roll over, displacing ripples of brown foam-flecked water, and malevolent eyes on the end of stalks would appear above the surface for a moment. Maurice offered the keeper half-a-crown.

"That's all right," he said. "You keep your money. I get paid, you know." It was most difficult to walk on the slimy surface and Maurice, who was exhausted from the afternoon's events, slipped and would have fallen had not the boy caught his arm. As he recovered his balance, he noticed Greta returning the keeper's amused smile. A moment later, a hippopotamus surfaced, blowing sprays of water from its great pink nostrils. Maurice's suit was flecked with mud.

"Sorry about that," said the keeper.

But Greta begged him not to worry. "It's a terrible old thing, anyway. I'm going to get him a new one to-morrow," she explained.

Maurice felt his throat fill with rage, anger that almost blinded him. He put his hands on her hips and in a moment he would have pushed her into the thick vaporous water; then he suddenly realized that he had no idea what would happen. Hippos, he felt sure, were not carnivorous, but in their anger at the disturbance they might destroy her, and that would be the end of both of them, he reflected with bitter satisfaction. On the other hand, they might just turn away from the floating Greta in disgust, in which case he would simply have mucked up all his schemes. He withdrew his hands in despair. Once again he had to control his fury.

Greta was most surprised when she felt his hands on her waist. How funny men were, she reflected, just when you thought you understood them, they did something unexpected like that. Maurice, who was always lecturing her for showing her affection in public! She was really rather touched by the gesture. All the same, she decided, it would be wiser not to notice it then. So turning her wide-eyed gaze up at him, "What *do* hippos eat, darling?" she asked in her childlike way.